HOLD THAT TIGER!

Remo felt the mistake in his chest. The nails tore flesh and cut into bones. He had treated this person as a busty, young, blonde woman—which was obviously wrong. He let out a scream of pain as the hand raked across his face, gouging nail slits into his cheeks. He felt his stomach spill from his torn belly with another swipe from the hissing creature.

But while the yellow-haired killer fought by instinct, Remo fought as man. Now, in full force, bleeding from his belly, terror in his throat, and his own death before his eyes, Remo, adopted son of Chiun, Master of Sinanju, struck back for the human race.

THE DESTROYER SERIES

The Destroyer

KILLER CHROMOSOMES #32

by Richard Sapir & Warren Murphy

PINNACLE BOOKS   LOS ANGELES

DESTROYER #32: KILLER CHROMOSOMES

Copyright © 1978 by Richard Sapir and Warren Murphy

All rights reserved, including the right to reproduce this book or portions thereof in any form.

An original Pinnacle Books edition, published for the first time anywhere.

ISBN: 0-523-40154-X

First printing, March 1978

Cover illustration by Hector Garrido

Printed in the United States of America

PINNACLE BOOKS, INC.
One Century Plaza
2029 Century Park East
Los Angeles, California 90067

For Sally Newmark

a gracious person,
a beautiful woman,
and the finest aunt in the whole world

KILLER CHROMOSOMES

CHAPTER ONE

They were afraid.

It was so small they couldn't see it with their naked eyes. It had yet to do them any harm. The nonscientists among them weren't even sure exactly what it did.

But 200 families from the greater Boston area, from as far away as Duxbury and even southern New Hampshire, pushed their way that rainy summer afternoon into the dirt and cement courtyard of the Boston Graduate School of Biological Sciences to protest against its manufacture.

"No. Not manufacture," explained an architect to one of the mothers. "They change it around but they don't make it new. Nobody can."

"Whatever," yelled the mother. "Stop them."

She knew what they were doing here at BGSBS was bad. They were making monsters that no one could stop. Horrible things like diseases no one could

1

cure, or mutations that would come into your bedroom and put their hairy hands all over you and lick you all over and do things to you. Maybe rape you. And then you would have that horror in your body.

Like the devil copulating with Mia Farrow in *Rosemary's Baby*, except here it could be real. They were so small, these things that could do the horrors, that they could enter your body without your even knowing it. Go right through your skin. You might not even have a blemish but you'd be dead.

And your babies would suffer worse. She liked the way one speaker had put it the night before at the pre-rally rally.

"I'm not going to tell you horror stories. I am not going to drag out some Bela Lugosi image out here in front of you. I am not going to use some scare tactics like telling you a mad scientist is laughing insanely over some bubbling test tube that is going to burn you all to death. I am simply going to give you a scientific fact: life, as you know it, is probably already over. You are probably already too late. We are not *going* to be doomed. We *are* doomed."

So that was it. Rationally and scientifically, any sane person would know life was over for good probably.

She saw the television cameramen from Channels 4 5, and 7 shooting down from the roof of the building and she saw great black cables stretching into a window on the third floor. That was where the evil scientists made those things and were going to try to prove they were harmless this day.

Harmless, she would give them harmless. How could something be harmless if everyone was already doomed? And if nothing else, it could ruin making babies. After all, they were using the same stuff to make babies.

A speaker rose on a small truck. He was a doctor. And he was worried.

2

"They are going to conduct their experiment today," he said. "They are going to take our their test tubes in their laboratory and show some five-minute expert from a newspaper or television station that what they are doing is safe. Well, it's not safe. And we're here to tell the world it is not safe. You don't tamper with the forces of life without danger. You let them make the atomic bomb and now you're living on the brink of nuclear holocaust. Well, the atomic bomb is child's play compared to this, because with an atomic bomb you know when it goes off. This damned thing could have gone off already and no one will know unless we tell them."

The speaker paused. Mrs. Walters loved the speakers in this movement. She cradled her pudgy child, Ethel, who was now dangerously moist. She was almost four but sometimes during great excitement accidents occurred. They had told all the mothers to bring their children and to make them as neat and as pretty as possible to show the world what they were trying to save. The children. The future. Tomorrow. That was it. They were simply saving tomorrow.

The thought made Mrs. Walters' eyes water. Something else was wet also. She shifted baby Ethel, who smiled contentedly at a television camera. The camera did not catch the moisture dripping down the mother's arms. Mrs. Walters tried to appear as loving as possible for the media while keeping baby Ethel away from the new print dress that might stain and stay stained.

The handheld camera came closer to her. A young man with beautifully structured hair and an immaculate suit and a very deep voice pushed a microphone in front of baby Ethel.

"And why are you here, child?"

"To stop the bad people," said Ethel. And the blue ribbons and the neat pigtails bobbed. Baby Ethel smiled. She had dimples.

3

"And you are?" asked the young announcer.

"Mrs. Walters. Mrs. Harry Walters of Haverhill, Massachusetts, and I'm here to protest what's going on here. I'm here to save tomorrow as the speaker just said."

"Save it from what?"

"From bad things," said Mrs. Walters. Baby Ethel reached out for the microphone. Mrs. Walters readjusted the heavy, wet bundle.

"Dr. Sheila Feinberg, the scientist who is conducting today's experiments, says that most of you don't even understand what she is doing."

"I don't understand how the atomic bomb works either but why on earth we ever made one, I'll never know."

"We were at war," explained the announcer.

"Oh, well, it was an immoral war. We had no business in Vietnam."

"We were at war with Germany and Japan."

"Now see how crazy that is," said Mrs. Walters. "They're such good friends. Why did we need an atomic bomb against good friends? We didn't need the bomb and we don't need Dr. Feinberg's plagues and monsters."

"What plagues? What monsters?"

"The worst kind," said Mrs. Walters righteously. "The kind you can't see or don't even know of."

The announcer repeated her name for the camera and sidled around the crowd to an entrance for newsmen and wondered how he could cut the crowd scenes down to twenty seconds. The station was attacking Boston potholes again and their humor announcer, who was as funny as prickly heat, was holding a special summer pothole contest that used up five minutes of air time every night. The whole station was like the *Titanic* where the band played as the ship went down. A New York firm gave them the snappiest theme song in the country and the station

4

provided the downright stupidest coverage of everything.

Dr. Sheila Feinberg was upstairs under the lights of a rival television station. The announcer waited for them to finish their interview. He felt suddenly very protective of this woman even though she was a scientist. She looked so out of place, sitting there under his channel's lights, waiting for a question. Like the plain, studious girls in school that you just knew would have to settle for some drip of a husband or never get married at all.

Dr. Feinberg, thirty-eight, had a strong, manly nose and a pinched, desperate sort of face, like an overworked accountant who had suddenly forgotten a key set of books and was about to lose a client over it.

She wore a loose, puffy, white blouse, which hid the absence of womanly roundness on her chest, and she had a skinny waist and wide hips under a dark-blue, flannel skirt. She wore plain black shoes with low heals. A desperate cameo brooch on the blouse proclaimed that she was a woman and had a right to wear such a thing, but it seemed as out of place as her new hairdo. It was a pert short cut, similar to one made famous by an ice skater, but on the ice skater it emphasized a cutesy-poo face. On Dr. Feinberg, it looked like a Christmas tree atop a tank turret—a desperately inappropriate piece of gaiety.

Softly, the announcer asked her to explain the demonstration and what she was doing. He also told her that it might be better if she didn't pick at her fingernails when she talked.

"What we're doing here," said Dr. Feinberg, with controlled softness that allowed neck veins to bulge like suddenly stepped-on, wrinkly blue balloons, "is exploring chromosomes. Chromosomes, genes, DNA,. are all part of the process that determines characteristics. It is why one seed becomes a petunia and another meets an egg and becomes Napoleon. Or Jesus.

5

Or Dr. Jonas Salk. What we're dealing with is the coding mechanism for what makes things the way they are."

"Your critics say that you could create a monster or a strange plague that could get out of the laboratory and destroy mankind."

Dr. Feinberg smiled sadly and shook her head.

"I call that the Frankenstein syndrome," she said. "You know how in the movies the mad scientist takes the brain of a criminal, puts it into pieces from many people's bodies and with lightning jolts the whole damned thing into something stranger than man? Well, if you followed that process you would have the biggest stink you could imagine. I doubt if you could get one percent of the tissue to live, much less perform, much less perform better than an average human being."

"Well, where do people get these ideas from?" asked the announcer.

"From stories and television. They see a man get in an accident and then some mechanical, electronic wizardry makes him stronger and better-seeing than any man alive. Well, that is not so. If I tried to put a bionic arm onto your shoulder you'd have lesions for ten years. It would be super tender, and if the arm by some mechanical skill is made stronger than the human arm, it would throw you around every time you tried to use it. I mean, it's ridiculous. Our problem is not keeping some monster under control but trying to get a very delicate substance to survive. And that's what I am going to show today."

"How?"

"By drinking it."

"Isn't that dangerous?"

"Yes," said Dr. Feinberg. "For the organism. If the exposure to air doesn't kill it, my saliva will. You have to understand we're talking about one of the lowliest of all bacteria. To it we attach chromosomes and

6

genes from other forms of life. In years, many years, if we've been both talented and lucky, we may understand the genetic causes of cancer, of hemophilia, of diabetes. We may be able to create inexpensive vaccines to save the lives of people who today will die. We may be able to create food plants that draw nitrogen from the air and no longer need expensive fertilizers. But that's years away and that's why this whole protest is so ridiculous. We're barely able to keep these organisms alive now. Most of our intricate machinery is painstakingly designed to keep everything at just the right temperature, just the right acidity. Those people out there are worried about it conquering the world, and we're worried about trying to keep it alive under intensive care."

It took two hours for the public demonstration to begin. The protestors insisted on placing who they wanted where they wanted. The mothers with the babies got the front rows, right near the television cameras. Not one camera could focus on the experiment without framing it with babys' faces.

The material was in a long, clear fishtank. There were twelve small, sealed test tubes submerged in clear liquid in the tank which was set on a black-topped table.

Dr. Feinberg asked everyone not to smoke.

"Why? Because then we'll see how vicious that stuff is? If it isn't dangerous, why do you have it cooped up in glass and water inside the glass?" called out one man.

"First, we don't have water in this tank. Water transmits variations of temperature too rapidly. We have a gelatin solution which acts as insulation. These are unstable elements."

"Unstable. It can blow up," yelled a bald man with a beard. He wore a single love bead on a gold strand around his neck.

"Unstable . . . it can die. That's what I mean," said Dr. Feinberg patiently.

"Liar," yelled out Mrs. Walters. Baby Ethel was positively rancid by now. The sweet dimples hid an odor that even the mother could not stand. It did not bother baby Ethel. She was used to it.

"No, you don't understand. It really is very sensitive. What we're trying to get, and we don't even have the correct combination yet, is a very delicate key."

"You're taking the seed of life," yelled out another person.

"No, no. Please listen. Do you know why, when you grow older, your nose stays your nose and your eyes stay your eyes? Even though every seven years every cell has been replaced?"

"Because you haven't had a chance to mess with it," shouted a man.

"No," said Dr. Feinberg, trembling. "Because there is a code system in your body that makes you *you*. And what we're doing here at Boston Biological is trying to find the key to that code, so that bad things like cancers won't reproduce themselves. We have in these test tubes genes of various animals treated with combinations of what we call unlocking elements. Hopefully we can produce variations that will help us understand why things are the way they are and how we can help ourselves to make them better. What we are working on here is the key to unlock closed doors between chromosome systems if you will."

"Rotten liar," yelled out someone and then the group began the chant of liar and finally someone challenged Dr. Feinberg to "touch the deadly fluid with your bare hands."

"Oh, come on," she said in disgust and reached into the tank. One woman shrieked and every mother shielded her child except Mrs. Walters, who let baby

Ethel fend her own smelly way. She waited to see Dr. Feinberg's hand disintegrate.

Out came a test tube. Clear, gooey stuff clung to Dr. Feinberg's hand.

"For those of you who like horror, I have in this test tube the genes from a man-eating tiger, treated with the unlocking mechanism. Man-eating tiger."

There were gasps from the audience. Dr. Feinberg shook her head sadly. She looked to the announcer who had been friendly. He smiled at the woman. He understood. There was nothing more terrible about man-eating tiger genes than about the genes of a mouse. Both of them could hardly survive outside their carriers. If they were not already dead anyway.

Dr. Feinberg drank the liquid in the test tube and made a face.

"Would anyone care to select another test tube?" she said.

"They're not real killer chromosomes," yelled someone and that was enough.

"You stupid, stupid, ignorant people," yelled Dr. Feinberg in frustration. "You won't understand."

Furiously, she rammed her hand into the gelatin insulated tank, snatched another bottle, and drank it. She drank another. She drooled and drank. She uncorked and drank. She finished every one of those test tubes and it all tasted vaguely like someone else's spit. And there she was.

"Here. What do you expect me to do, change into Wolfman? You ignorant, ignorant people."

And then she shivered. And her short haircut shivered. And, like an old bolt of cloth, she collapsed to the ground.

"Don't touch her. She might be contagious," yelled baby Ethel's mother.

"Idiots," snapped the announcer for the TV station, breaking his code of impartiality. He called an ambulance and after the unconscious Dr. Feinberg was taken out in a stretcher, still breathing, one of her colleagues explained it was unfortunate she passed out because he was sure the genetic matter she swallowed could not have caused even an upset stomach. She had passed out from the excitement, he said.

"I mean, it is improbable that the genetic material had anything to do with it," he said.

But no one listened. One of the leaders of the protesting group jumped on the lab table near the fishtank.

"Touch nothing. This place is contaminated." When he had silence and was sure the cameras had stopped panning the milling crowd, he waved his arms and spoke.

"Nothing could happen, they told us. Nothing could harm anyone, they told us. The genes and chromosomes and whatever life codes these monsters are tinkering with have trouble enough surviving, they said. Well, at least this time it has struck only the guilty. Let's stop it before it strikes the innocent."

The protestors, reveling in their good fortune, continued their meeting long after the news cameramen had left. Babies become cranky and someone was sent out for infant's formula. Someone else was dispatched for hamburgers and soft drinks for the elders. They passed fourteen resolutions, all numbered, all labeled Boston Graduate Biological. In this way, the resolution itself would always bring up the accident that happened in the lab where no accident could happen.

Baby Ethel went to sleep in her moist pants, soiled backside up, unsmiling face down on her mother's rolled-up jacket in the rear of the laboratory.

Someone thought they saw a figure paw toward her. Someone else looked around to hear a very low, grumbling growl that seemed to come from just outside the window leading to the alley. And then a young child wandered through saying Dr. Feinberg had returned.

10

"The lady who drank the nasty things," said the child in explanation.

"Oh, God. No," came a voice from the back of the room. "No, no, no."

Mrs. Walters knew baby Ethel was sleeping back there. She bulled her way through the group, knocking over chairs and people, following a mother's instinct as old as the caves. She knew something bad had come to her child. She slipped, slamming into the person who had cried out in horror. She tried to get up but slipped again. She was wallowing in some oily, red goo. It wasn't oily. It was slippery. It was blood.

She was on her knees trying to get to her feet when she saw the extraordinary pale face of baby Ethel so deeply, peacefully, in sleep despite the screaming. Then the woman who called out stepped aside and Mrs. Walters saw her baby had no stomach, as if it had been eaten out, and the little body had let its blood out all over the floor.

"Oh, God," sobbed Mrs. Walters. "No. No. No. No."

She reached out for the loose head of her baby but she could not keep her balance while kneeling and slipped again.

The ambulance that was supposed to have taken Dr. Feinberg to the hospital was found with its front twisted around a tree trunk on Storrow Drive. One driver dead with his throat torn out and the other babbling.

Detectives pieced together that the last passenger was Dr. Feinberg. She had been in a coma, but now she was not in the wrecked ambulance. Whoever had killed the driver had taken her. There was blood in the front seat. There was no blood in the back. The attendant who lived had a single deep gash near his forehead.

The forensic surgeon asked if they were going to return the attendant to the zoo. He said the attendant should go back because if he carried that fear of animals with him for long, the animals would know it.

"He'd better go back tomorrow or he'll never go back at all. He'll be too afraid. That's what I'm saying. I've treated claw wounds before," the surgeon said.

"He didn't work in no zoo," said the detective. "He was an ambulance attendant who was knifed. He didn't work in no zoo."

"That on the head is a claw mark," said the doctor. "No knife cuts like that. A knife doesn't rip like that. That's puncture, then rip."

When the corpse of baby Ethel came in on another case, the doctor was sure there was a big cat loose in the city.

"Look at the belly," he said.

"There isn't any belly," said the detective.

"That's what I mean. Big cats eat the belly first. It's the best part. If you ever see a calf, the big cats will eat the belly. The humans eat the steaks from the rump. That's why I say it was a big cat. Unless, of course, you know somebody who's going around collecting human intestines."

In a dark loft in Boston's North End, Sheila Feinberg trembled, clutching a rafter. She did not want to think of the blood on her and the horror of someone else dying and that there was somebody else's blood on her body. She did not even want to open her eyes. She wanted to die, right there in the dark, and not think about what happened.

She was not a religious person, never understanding the language in which her father had prayed. Even if she had, by the age of twelve she felt quite secure in believing there was an order to things and people should be moral because it was right, not because they had to do right to be rewarded later on.

Thus, she did not know how to pray. Until this night, when she prayed that God, or whatever there was that ran the universe, would take her from this horror.

Her knees and forearms rested on the rafter. The floor was fifteen feet below. She felt safer on this perch, almost invulnerable. And she could see very well now, of course.

A small movement in the corner. A mouse. No, she thought. Too small for a mouse.

She cleaned her hands of the blood by licking them and a feeling of goodness came upon her body.

Her chest and throat rumbled.

She purred.

She was happy again.

CHAPTER TWO

His name was Remo and the man was throwing a punch at him. He was actually throwing a punch. Remo watched it.

Years before, a punch had been something fast that you ducked or blocked or saw suddenly at the end of a fist banging into your head with hurt.

Now it was almost ridiculous.

There was this very big man. He was six feet-four inches tall. He had big shoulders and big arms, a very big chest and drive-hammer thighs. He wore oil-covered dungarees, a checkered shirt and thick hobnailed boots. He worked driving cut-down trees, forest to mill in Oregon, and no, he wasn't going to stay for another twenty minutes at the Eatout Diner stop just so some old gook could finish writing some letter. The faggy guy in the black T-shirt had better haul that dinky yellow car out of the way or he would run it over.

No?

"Well then, skinny man, I'm going to pulverize you," said the log driver.

And then the punch started. The man was much bigger than Remo, outweighing him by more than a hundred pounds. The man awkwardly set his balance and started his bulk toward Remo, bringing a big, hairy fist ponderously around from behind him, driving with his legs and throwing his whole body into the blow. People from the diner ran out to see the skinny fellow with the foreigner get murdered by Houk Hubbley who had already put more men in the hospital than you could shake a Homelite chain saw at.

Waiting for the punch, Remo pondered his options. There was nothing miraculous about it. A few top hitters could see the seams of a baseball as it whizzed toward them from the pitcher. Basketball players could feel hoops they could not see. And skiers could hear the consistency of snow they had not yet skied on.

These people did it with natural talent that had accidentally been developed to a minor degree. Remo's skills had been worked, reworked, honed, and blossomed under the tutelage of more than three thousand years of wisdom so that while average persons with deadened senses saw blurs, Remo saw knuckles and bodies moving, not in slow motion, but almost in still photographs.

There was big Houk Hubbley threatening. There was the crowd coming out to see Remo get pulverized and then began the long, slow punch.

In the back of the yellow Toyota, Chiun, the Master of Sinanju, with skin as wrinkled as parchment and wisps of white hair gracing his frail-appearing head, leaned over a writing pad, his long-plumed goose quill pen scratching away. He was creating a great saga of love and beauty.

16

Chiun had trained Remo. He therefore had every right to expect peace and quiet and that undue noise should not be made while he was composing his thoughts. First he imagined the great love affair between the king and the courtesan and then he penned the words.

The only thing he wanted from outside the car was quiet. Remo realized this and as the punch came, like a slow train rumbling into a station, Remo gently put his right hand under the oncoming arm. So that the man would not grunt loudly, Remo compressed the lungs evenly by thrusting his left arm across the stomach and his left knee behind the back so that big Houk Hubbley looked as if he suddenly had a skinny human pretzel wrapped around him.

Houk Hubbley felt explosively peaked. He had swung and now he was out of breath. With his right fist held up in the air, and like a statue that could not move, he was falling on that hand, and by jiminy, the hand was being forced open, changing from a fist, to catch his body, and he was rolling on the ground, out of breath, and there was a foot on his throat, a black loafer with green gum on its sole to be exact, and the guy in the gray flannels and the black shirt was standing over him.

"Shhhh," whispered Remo. "You get air for quiet. Quiet for air. It's a trade, sweetheart."

The man didn't say all right but Remo knew he meant all right. His body meant it. Remo let some air into the man's lungs as the big face reddened. Then like kicking on an engine, Remo compressed the lungs gently once more and they opened full, sucking in a large and blessed supply of oxygen for Houk Hubbley, who lay there still on the diner driveway.

Hearing the sucking gasp of air, Chiun looked up from his writing pad.

"Please," he said.

"Sorry," said Remo.

17

"Not everyone can write a love story," he said.

"Sorry," said Remo.

"When a man gives the wisdom of the ages to a coarse gruntling, the least the gruntling can do is keep a certain quiet about places where important things are being done."

"I said I'm sorry, Little Father."

"Sorry, sorry, sorry," mumbled Chiun. "Sorry for this and sorry for that. Propriety does not require a sorry. Correctness means never having to say you're sorry."

"So I'm not sorry," said Remo. "I'm out here tending this guy so he won't make noise, stopping him from starting his truck so it won't make noise, because I want you to be disturbed. See? I'm cunning about it. I'm not sorry at all. Never have been. I'm inconsiderate."

"I knew that," said Chiun. "Now I cannot write."

"You haven't written for a month on that thing. You just stare at it, day after day. You're using everything for an excuse. I stopped that truck and this guy just so you'll face the fact that you're not a writer."

"There are no good love stories around today. The great day dramas of your television have degenerated into nothing. They have violence, even sex. This is a pure love story. Not cows and bulls reproducing. But love. I understand love because I know and care enough not to disturb people at productive work."

"Not for a month, Little Father. Not a word."

"Because you make noise."

"No noise," said Remo.

"Noise," said Chiun and tore up the pad with a flurry of his sharp fingernails. He slid his hands into the sleeves of the opposite arms of his kimono. "I cannot compose while you carp."

Remo massaged Houk Hubbley's chest with his foot. Hubbley felt a lot better. Well good enough to

18

get to his feet. Good enough to take another poke at the skinny guy.

Skinny guy hardly noticed him. Just a little bit. Enough to be where the punch was not.

It was the strangest thing. Skinny guy didn't duck, didn't dodge, didn't block a punch. Just wasn't there when the fist was.

"Even if you got it down on paper, which you won't, nobody's interested in love stories in this country. They want sex."

"There is nothing new to sex," said Chiun. "Sex does not change from emperor to peasant, from Pharaoh to your cab drivers. Babies are made very much the same as they have always been made."

"Well, still Americans like to read about it."

"Why? Can't they do it? You people seem to breed well enough. There are so many of you. Almost all of you with meat on your breath and insults on your tongue, making noise."

"You want to sell a book, Little Father, write about sex."

"That takes up less than one page," said Chiun, his eyebrows furrowing in worry. "The seed meets the egg and a baby happens. Or the seed does not meet the egg and a baby does not happen. This is a subject for a book? The white mind is mysterious."

Remo turned back to Hubbley who was still throwing punches. The crowd on the diner steps now was cheering Remo on and laughing at Hubbley.

"Enough. No more games," said Remo to Hubbley.

"All right, you sumbitch, I'll show you what no more games is."

Big Houk Hubbley went to the cab of his truck. From underneath the seat, he pulled out a sawed-off shotgun. It could shiver a telephone pole in two. Or mutilate a wall. At close range, sawed-off shotguns made people chopped liver.

The folks on the porch stopped laughing at Houk

19

Hubbley. That made him feel better. That was what he wanted. Respect. And he was going to get it from that skinny fellow too.

"Put that away," said Remo mildly. "You can hurt with that. That's not nice playing."

"Apologize," said Houk Hubbley. So he would do a few years in the state pen if he had to for sausaging the guy. So what? Lots of loggers had done time. Time didn't make a man no different. Time nowadays was just about the same as not doing time, now that they had you out in the forests working. You could also get yourself a woman in prison if you had the right connections and you kept your smarts. So why not kill the guy? Unless, of course, he apologized.

But then an even stranger thing happened. Sure, it was mighty peculiar that the skinny guy couldn't be hit by a punch. Not even right up close, sometimes so close the knuckles felt the black T-shirt and they had the chest right there in the path of a good punch and then it was gone. That was peculiar enough, but now something even weirder happened. And Houk Hubbley would swear for many a year afterward that this thing really happened.

As soon as he had decided he was going to pull the trigger, without saying anything different, without making any special move, the old Oriental lifted his head as if he were a mind reader. The skinny white guy stopped his conversation with the Oriental and also looked. At the very same time, as if both of them knew instantly what had gone on inside Houk Hubbley's mind.

"No," said the white guy. "Better not."

Houk Hubbley didn't threaten, didn't smile, just stood there with his right trigger finger cradling that deadly strip of metal that could send a wall of shot out at the yellow Toyota and the two men.

It was a quiet moment. Then suddenly the old gook wasn't in the seat anymore and Houk Hubbley could swear all he did was try to get a peek at where the old guy was and then he didn't see anything.

There was this bright light up above and this fellow with a green mask and the place smelled of ether. If this was the diner driveway, why was there a ceiling above him? His back was on a very hard thing and someone was talking to a nurse, and there were now three people with green masks and green caps looking down at him and someone was saying something about a local anesthetic and someone was coming to.

Houk Hubbley realized that it was he who was coming to. The people looking down at him were doctors. He could hear their problem. Something about rectal canals. And two unfired shells in the chamber. And the trigger guard being inside. They would have to cut to it, because a yank might explode the shells.

And then a doctor noticed Houk was aware of what was going on.

"Mister," he said, "would you mind telling us how you got a sawed-off shotgun, loaded, into your intestinal tract? I mean, how did you do it without the thing going off? I know this model. It's got a hair trigger. How did you do it?"

"You won't believe it but I think it was because I had a nasty thought."

In downtown Portland, Remo waited by a telephone booth, looking at his watch. He did not need it to tell time but he needed it to make sure that upstairs was telling time correctly. In one hand he had a dime and in the other hand he had a telephone number. He was no good at this code thing and the only time it worked for people was when they were code people themselves. Remo suspected that every intelligence agency or secret organization had a code nut. Nobody else understood what the code nut was up to, except other code nuts, often in competing services. These code nuts made their codes more and more

21

complicated to prevent other code nuts on the other side from understanding them.

Meanwhile, the people who had to use those things went stumbling along, guessing at what was what. If Remo understood what upstairs wanted, then the third number in the telephone number was the number of times he should let the number ring before phoning back and the fourth number was the time of day he should phone. The third number was two and the fourth number was five.

Remo made a mental bet with himself. The bet was three to one he would not reach upstairs correctly.

A man with a blue snap-brimmed hat and eyeglasses was using the phone. He carried a cane over his arm.

"Sir," said Remo. "I'm in sort of a rush. Would you let me use the phone, please?"

The man shook his head. He said to someone on the other end of the line to go ahead, he was in no hurry.

Remo hung up for him. He wedged the head and the hat between phone box and wall. The eyeglasses popped up to the man's eyebrows. He grunted. He could not make clear sounds because his jaw was wedged open. He sounded like he was in a dentist's chair.

Remo dialed the number, waited for two rings, hung up and dialed again. He was sure it wasn't going to work.

"Yes," came the acidic voice. It had worked.

Remo unwedged the man's head.

"Sorry," he said. "You're going to have to hobble away. I need privacy. I didn't think I'd reach my party, but you know, I did. Thanks."

He gave the man back his cane and told him to work his jaw and the pain would go away.

"Who was that?" asked the voice on the other end of the line. The voice was that of Harold W. Smith, head of CURE, and to Remo, a man who worried too much about too many things.

"Somebody who got his head caught between the phone and a wall."

"This is not the sort of conversation that should be carried on in public."

"I'm alone. He's gone."

"Did you kill him?"

"What is this? C'mon. What's the message?"

"You might not want to leave so many bodies around."

Remo quickly scribbled on a pad. This new system for messages was supposed to have been simplified so that he could understand it. By transposing words instead of letters and every word at a different integer on his card, to be translated into another word, he was now supposed to be able to get quickly and easily a coded message that no one else could interpret.

He had the card and his pencil out, along with a piece of notepaper.

He put the message together.

"What do you want me to do in Albuquerque?"

"That wasn't the message," said Smith. "Here is the message."

"Jerk," mumbled Remo.

"Blue bellies Boston Globe 19 and Zebra. Got it?"

"Yep," said Remo.

"Does it make sense?"

"Not at all," said Remo. "Not even slightly."

"All right. Fifty-four dancers break three dowels."

"Gotcha," said Remo. "I'll be there."

He hung up and put the code card in his rear pocket. It looked like a bank calendar with descriptions of very peculiar loan rates. He was to meet Smith at the Logan Airport shuttle room in Boston.

Chiun was in the Toyota. He was busy not writing his tale of the king's love. How could he be expected

23

to compose beauty with Remo ramming dimes into a telephone?

"We're going to Boston," said Remo.

"That is the other side of your country."

"Right."

"How can I write when we go shifting from one side of this country to another?" asked Chiun.

On the flight to Boston, he mentioned seven times how a true artist could not write while travelling, how if he were not travelling he would have completed his novel by now, how this was the very best time to write and it might never come again. If it weren't for this trip and its chaos, he would have done the book. Now it was over forever. Because of Remo.

Not that Chiun was in the habit of blaming, he mentioned. He just wanted things understood. He was not blaming Remo but Remo might just as well have set fire to Chiun's manuscript, a manuscript that probably was superior to William Shakespeare's, a famous white writer. Chiun mentioned famous white writers because if he mentioned Hak Lo, Remo would ask who Hak Lo was.

Remo wasn't asking who Hak Lo was. A man with a big grin, a checkered suit, and a gold keychain adorning his expanse of suede vest, apologized for listening into someone else's conversation but could the fine gentleman in the kimono possibly tell him who Hak Lo was? He was interested and did not know.

Remo put the man's unfinished luncheon compote, served in plastic dishes by the stewardesses, into the man's grinning face. Not hard. But the plastic bowl did crack.

It was not asked again on the flight across the continent who Hak Lo was.

Remo remained happily unknowing.

At Logan Airport in Boston, Chiun quoted a few lines from Hak Lo:

"Oh, torpid blossom
That meanders through thine unctuous morning,
Let thy perambulant breezes cusp,
Like the dalliance of a last-breathed life."

"That," Chiun said proudly, "is Hak Loian."

"That is icky mess," said Remo.

"You are a barbarian," said Chiun. His voice was high and squeaky, angrier than normal.

"Because I don't like what I don't like. I don't care if you think America is such a new backward country. My opinion is as good as anyone else's. Anyone's. Especially yours. You're just an assassin like me. You're no better."

"Just an assassin?" asked Chiun, overwhelming horror seizing him. He stopped. The fold of the light blue kimono fluttered like a tree being hit by one sudden gust of breeze. They were at the entrance to the shuttle terminal of Logan Airport.

"Just an assassin?" Chiun shrieked in English. "More than a decade of the millenia of wisdom, poured into an unworthy white vessel, a stupid white vessel that calls an assassin just an assassin. There are just poets and there are just kings and there are just wealthy men. There are never just assassins."

"Just," said Remo.

People in their rush to catch their hourly flights to New York City stopped to look. Chiun's arms waved and the grace of the kimono flowed like a flag in a wind tunnel.

Remo, whose casual balance and strong face tended to weaken most women, often with desires they had not known they had, looked even sharper and turned like a cat toward Chiun.

And there they argued.

Dr. Harold W. Smith, whose public identity was as the director of Folcroft Sanitarium, the cover for the organization and home of its massive computer banks, looked over his neatly folded New York Times at the two men fighting, one his lone killer arm, the other his Oriental trainer, and regretted meeting in a public place.

So secret was the organization only one man, Remo, was allowed to kill and only Smith, each American president and Remo himself knew exactly what the organization did. More often than not, the organization would pass up a necessary mission because of fear of exposure. Secrecy was more important for CURE than for the CIA because the CIA was constitutionally licensed to operate. But CURE had been set up in violation of the Constitution to do things.

And now, with terror as deep as the marrow of his bones, Smith watched his killer arm loudly talking about assassins. And just in case anyone should not be interested, there was Chiun, the Master of Sinanju and the most recent descendant of a line of more than 2,000 years of master assassins, in Oriental garb, screaming, his parchment face red. Screaming about assassins. Smith wanted to crawl into the pages of his *New York Times* and disappear.

A highly rational man, he understood that most people would not comprehend that the two were really killers. And they had ways of getting through people and official forces that was miraculous.

The danger now was that Smith would be seen talking to Remo. He would have to abort this mission.

He folded his newspaper and blended himself into the line of passengers headed toward New York. He turned his head away from the arguing pair who had not seen him. He looked out at the airport runways beneath this circular terminal for the shuttle flights. He became quite interested in the smog over Boston.

He was almost at the ramp to the plane when he felt a tap on his shoulder. It was Remo.

"No, I don't have a match," said Smith. This would let Remo know that everything was off. Smith could not afford to be identified with such an attention-drawing scene as Remo had just irresponsibly created.

"C'mon, Smitty," said Remo.

To stand there and deny he knew Remo would draw even more attention.

Feeling as though his blood was drained from his limbs, Smith got out of the line. He ignored Chiun's formal sweeping bow and kept walking. All three got into a cab to Boston.

"Everyone can have half fare if it's a group fare. It's cheaper," said the cabbie.

"Quiet," said Smith.

For the first time, Remo noticed how Smith's gray suit and vest were so confining. He had never thought the man needed to be unconfined. Probably the only baby born with constipation and a sour disposition.

"And that goes for you two also," Smith said. "Quiet. Please."

"Listen," said the cabbie. "This is our new community rate to bring you, the community, a more equitable transportation service within the economic grasp of all."

"That's pretty good," said Remo.

"I thought so," said the cabbie.

"Do you use your ears?"

"Yes."

"Then use them now. I'm not going to give you that rate. But if you interrupt me again, I'm going to put your earlobes in your lap. This is a very sincere promise," said Remo.

"Remo!" said Smith sharply. The bloodless face paled even more.

"Merely an assassin," said Chiun, staring at the grit and brick of north-end Boston. "There are a hundred thousand doctors, most of whom will do you harm, but they are not just doctors."

27

Remo looked at Smith and shrugged. "I don't know what you're getting upset about."

"Very many things," said Smith. "You've been creating problems."

"Life's a problem," said Remo.

"Every country has a king or a president or an emperor. Never has there been a country without one. Yet few have good assassins, a blessing and a rarity. Who talks of just an emperor? When indeed, it is truly just an emperor. An emperor is merely an untrained person who usually did nothing more than be correctly born. But an assassin . . . ah, the training. For a real assassin," said Chiun.

"I don't want to talk about this in public," said Smith. "That's one of our problems."

"Not mine," said Remo.

"Any idiot can write a book," said Chiun. "That is no great accomplishment when one has time and is not bothered by noisy whites. But who says just a writer? Anyone can write given quiet and no disturbances. But an assassin . . ."

"Please. Both of you," said Smith.

"Both what?" asked Remo.

"Chiun was talking also," said Smith.

"Oh," said Remo.

Hearing that he should keep quiet, Chiun turned his frail head to Smith. Although normally excessively polite to anyone who employed the House of Sinanju, this time was another matter. Every few centuries there was an emperor loose-tongued enough to tell a Master of Sinanju to be quiet. It was not the wisest move and was never repeated. Giving loyalty was one thing, allowing abuse another.

Smith saw Chiun's stare, that incredibly deep quiet. It was beyond a threat. It was as if for the first time Smith had been exposed to the terrible, awesome force of the tiny, old Oriental, because he had stepped over some invisible line.

Smith had faced death before and had been afraid, yet faced it and did what he had to do.

It was not fear he felt this time, looking at the stillness of the Master of Sinanju. It was like being naked and unprepared in the face of creation. It was like Judgment Day and he was wrong. He had gone into a wrong place because he had made that incredible mistake of taking the Master of Sinanju lightly and for granted.

"I'm sorry," said Smith. "I apologize."

Chiun did not answer right away. It seemed like ages to Smith but finally the old head bowed, indicating the apology was accepted. Somehow an apology was not necessary for Remo. Smith could not explain it but it was so.

In a small restaurant, Smith ordered a meal. Remo and Chiun said they wanted nothing. Smith ordered the cheapest spaghetti and meatballs then waved a chrome rod around the table.

"No bugs," he said. "I guess we're safe. Remo, I am vastly unhappy about the public way, the attention-attracting way you're doing your job."

"Okay, then let's call it a day. I've been with you, doing work that no other man could do, too, too long. Too many hotel rooms, too many Ping Pong codes, too many emergencies and too many places where no one knows me."

"It's not that simple, Remo," Smith said. "We need you. Your country needs you. I know that matters to you."

"Horse spit," said Remo. "That doesn't matter to me at all. The only person who ever gave me anything in my life is . . . I'm not going to go into it," said Remo. "But it ain't you, Smitty."

Chiun smiled. "Thank you," he said.

"What can I say?" asked Smith. "Other than, you know, things are not going well for your country. We've had hard times."

"So have I," said Remo.

"I don't know how to put this and I am really at a loss for words," Smith said. "We not only need you but we need you in a special manner. You have been attracting attention and we can't afford it."

"How?" said Remo belligerently.

"For instance. There was a television short on the news last night. Someone had given some pottery maker out in Portland, Oregon, a yellow Toyota. Ownership papers and everything. Because he didn't feel like parking it. And he was with an old Oriental."

"Old?" questioned Chiun. "Is the mighty oak old because it is not a green, sap-spewing twig?"

"No," said Smith. "Sorry, but that's what television said." He turned back to Remo. "Now I know you just gave that Toyota away. I know it was you. You bought it to drive around and then you got to the airport and you didn't feel like parking it, so you gave it to some good-looking woman who was passing by."

"What should I have done? Drive it into the Pacific? Burn it? Explode it?"

"You should have done something that wouldn't get some news announcer talking about 'How's this for a great Mother's Day gift, folks?'"

"We were late for the plane."

"Park it or sell it for fifty dollars."

"You ever try selling a car worth several thousand dollars for fifty dollars? No one would buy it. They wouldn't trust it."

"Or the scene in the airport lounge," said Smith.

"Yes. This time I must agree with our most beautiful Emperor Smith," said Chiun who called anyone who employed him "emperor." "He is right. What insanity prompted you in a public place before a multitude of people to say 'just an assassin'? How could you have done such an irresponsible and thoughtless thing? Pray tell. What? Explain yourself, Remo."

Remo didn't answer. He made a motion with his hands that he wanted to hear the assignment.

He heard the story of Dr. Sheila Feinberg and how people were killed as if by a tiger.

"Two deaths don't really bother us," said Smith. "That's not the worry."

"It never is," said Remo bitterly.

"What makes this different is that human beings, the human race as we now know it, might just be facing extinction."

The spaghetti and meatballs came and Smith was quiet. When the waiter was gone, Smith continued.

"We have defense mechanisms in our bodies that fight diseases. Our best minds believe that whatever transformed Dr. Feinberg has broken down those defense mechanisms. Basically what we're talking about is a microbe more deadly than a nuclear weapon."

Chiun smoothed his robe. Remo noticed the paintings in this restaurant were done on the wall. The artist had used a lot of green.

"We don't think the police can properly handle it. You've got to isolate this Dr. Feinberg, then isolate what she has apparently accidentally discovered. Otherwise, I think mankind is going under."

"It's been going under since we climbed out of the trees," Remo said.

"Worse this time. Those animal genes shouldn't have affected her. But they did. Somehow there was an unlocking process which enabled different genes to mix. Now if that can be done, then there's no telling what might happen. There might be a disease for which man has no immunity. Or there might be a race created much stronger than man. Remo, I mean it. This whole thing is perhaps more menacing to mankind than anything that's ever happened in the history of the species."

"You know they put sugar in that tomato sauce,"

said Remo, pointing to the white strands of pasta buried under a rich red mound of tomato sauce.

"Maybe you haven't heard what I said but you two should know this thing could destroy the world. Including Sinanju," said Smith.

"I beg your pardon, I didn't hear you," said Chiun. "Would you repeat the last sentence, please, oh, Gracious Emperor?"

CHAPTER THREE

Captain Bill Majors had heard propositions before but never one so direct from someone who looked so unprofessional.

"Look, honey," he said. "I don't pay for it."

"Free," said the woman. She was skinny, closing in on forty, and pretty well level from shoulder to navel. But she had big, brown, catlike eyes and she seemed so intense. And, what the heck, Bill Major's wife was back in North Carolina. And Bill Majors was one of the top men in Special Forces which meant, to Captain Majors, experienced at hand-to-hand combat, he had nothing to fear from anyone. And besides, he might be doing the girl a favor. She looked as if she really needed a man.

He whispered in her ear, "Okay, honey. You can eat me if you want. Your place or mine?"

Her name was Sheila, she said, and she seemed quite furtive, looking over her shoulder every few moments, hiding her face from policemen who passed, letting the captain pay for the hotel room at the Copley Plaza with her money. She just didn't want the clerk to see her.

They got a room facing Copley Square. Trinity Church was on their right when they looked out the window. Captain Majors pulled the shades.

He took off his clothes and rested his knuckles on his bare hips.

"Okay," he said. "You said you wanted to eat me, now go ahead."

Sheila Feinberg smiled.

Captain Bill Majors smiled.

His smile was sexual but hers was not.

Sheila Feinberg did not take off her clothes. She kissed Majors on his hairy chest, then she put a tongue on the chest. The tongue was moist. The skin of the chest was soft. It covered bone and muscle. Bone rich in marrow for tooth cracking, and rich, red human blood. Rich like fresh whipped cream over warm cinnamon apple used to be.

But this was better.

Sheila opened her mouth. She licked the chest, then ran the edges of her teeth along the flesh.

She could restrain herself no longer. Down came the teeth with a beautiful mouthful of human flesh. She yanked it free with a snap of her neck.

Bill Majors suffered immediate shock. His hand went down on her neck, but it was a reflexive and weak blow. He beat at her hard but one did not generate much strength when incisors had gone through one's ventricle valves.

From hip to sternum, Bill Majors' stomach cavity was cleaned out to the last spinal lick.

In an elevator going down in Copley Plaza, someone saw a woman whose dress was covered with blood and offered to help her. But the woman refused.

Sheila ducked through a basement into an alley.

She knew she couldn't continue like this and yet she knew she could not stop going on like this.

She was quite rational, having developed that talent in lieu of the beauty which she knew she would never have.

She was no longer the biologist, no longer the daughter of Sol and Ruth Feinberg who had gone out on hundreds of blind dates on which she had been described as "a nice girl." A "nice girl" in her social circle was someone who didn't put out and whose looks made that job easy.

She was no longer the brilliant director of Boston Biological.

She was no longer the resident of Jamaica Plains with the new two-bedroom duplex, the Mediterranean furniture and the big couch overlooking the Jamaicaway, that she thought Mr. Right might use when he came along to begin that first beautiful seduction.

Technically, she was not a virgin, having experienced a man once. For Sheila Feinberg, it was a messy experience and she knew that great big wonderful excitement she had been promised was over when the man kept asking, "Was it good for you? Was it good?"

"Yeah," Sheila had said. But it was not good. And she did not like herself afterward. And later, while she continuously thirsted for the release of sex, she accepted the fact that, barring some miracle—hopefully with the pediatrician in her building who had just gotten divorced and smiled at her every morning—she would thirst until her body wants dried with age. Perhaps that was why she was drawn to genetic research and the coding that made one sperm into man and the other into tiger.

Now, as she padded through the alley, her dress front bloodied, she felt the release of not wanting a man sexually. And, having that release, she understood how the previous person, the one called Sheila

Feinberg, had suffered from the want of a man. It was like a tight shoe being taken off; it was not the sexual release she had read about; it was simply no longer a desire.

She was not in heat.

She just didn't want it anymore.

She wanted to eat and sometime, in the proper season, mate and bear children. But her children. Not the grandchildren of Sol and Ruth, but the litter Sheila. They would know how to stalk their prey. She would teach them.

Boston in the spring, she thought. So many, many delicious people. She had not returned to her apartment, nor had she phoned her co-workers at Boston Biological. They were people. They would, when they understood who and what she had become, try to destroy her. People were like that.

And her mind, still inordinately rational, told her the human race would send its best hunters after her. And with the instinct of everything from man to amoeba, that one element shared by every living thing, the instinct of survival of the species, Sheila knew she must first live and then reproduce.

People on the street offered to help her and she realized she had been too slow in recollecting that a dress front covered with blood was different and drew attention.

Was that changing in her head also? Was she losing the human sense of propriety? She would need that to survive among humans.

Just as she would need her experiments.

She ducked into a small antique shop. The owner offered to call an ambulance. She said she didn't need it. She cuffed the owner into unconsciousness and locked the door. She heard a baby cry and she did not think of swaddling it. Instead, she thought that she was not hungry at the moment.

And, realizing that, and not feeling for the human

baby, but with concern only for the new species that she had become, Sheila Feinberg realized in the dusty antique shop with the owner unconscious behind the counter that the last link with people had been severed.

She made a list of how to survive. Individually, people without weapons were generally defenseless. As a group, the human had no match on earth.

Until now.

Her features could very easily be identified.

She needed new features.

In the human, the male was usually the killer. She would give herself features that would disarm him.

Her hand was still steady and she was pleased with her thinking which she had feared she would lose. But as the list grew and darkness descended on Boston in the spring, she realized she was even more cunning than she had been.

Breasts. She underlined the word. Hair: blonde. Waist: slim. Hips: ample. Legs: long. The big breasts would be used to lure the male of the human species.

She had either by acute rationality or by instinct returned to the laboratory the first night to get and to hide away equipment. The first night had been very confusing. She remembered darkness coming on her as she drank all the combinations. She remembered being carted in something, then realizing it was an ambulance and when the attendant reached down to her, she saw his throat and was at it before she knew what she had done.

Biologically, it was quite clear what had happened. The human body replaced its cells every seven years. The billions of cells were changed. But why didn't a person change with the cells? Why did a nose come back as the same nose and the ears come back as the same ears and the minute fingerprints come back as the same fingerprints?

There was a coding system. The genes did more

37

than send lifetime messages through sperm and egg. They were a continuous living program. Like a record. So that as long as it played, Beethoven's Fifth could never become Elton John. But melt down the material, recast the record and you could have anything.

She had discovered the way to break down the record grooves of the cells and recast them during lifetime play. Through the combination of genes and the insulation material to keep them surviving, she had discovered the recasting method.

Whether or not it would take seven years to completely remake herself, she did not know. But in the meantime she had to live, and to live, she had to become someone other than Dr. Sheila Feinberg, homely, old maid scientist. She had to become someone that no one had ever seen before.

The materials from the lab were stuffed into a corner between the ceiling and beam in the warehouse in which she had hidden herself that first terrifying night. The scientist in her had lived through that transformation. And the transformation had been rapid. She was pretty sure why.

She had been highly excited. The body had been heated up, adrenalin was pumping at maximum flow, and the process took place in a faster-moving bloodstream.

The baby cried again, and now she needed it. It was untended for long periods, she deduced. Into an alley behind the antique store, she padded. She liked the night. The cry came from the second floor. Her hand fastened on a fire escape grate and slowly with one hand she pulled herself up.

Her logic told her this feat was far beyond anything she had ever been able to do before when she was fully human. If she could only get grasshopper genes. They would be far superior per ounce to those of a large cat. A grasshopper jumped more than

38

twenty times its own height, a tiger rarely more than three times its length. Humans? They were almost worthless. Pound for pound, the human was one of the worst creatures physically. Mentally however it excelled.

And the *Species Sheila Feinberg?* It would be something totally different. And it would have the whole world for its own.

The baby had gone back to sleep. It was very pink and it had been a half day since Sheila had eaten. But her rationality was still in control. She would have to hold onto that. She could not eat this morsel.

She flicked a piece of flesh from the side of the baby's eyes. The sting made it cry. Sheila backed into the shadows lest the human mother enter. There might be the father in the house. There might even be a gun.

No one came.

Sheila placed the baby flesh in the key solution that, when later combined with the laboratory insulation, would become the substance that could change the human recording. The baby flesh went into her mouth.

The substance was saliva. That was the secret key, the thing that had enabled the tiger genes Sheila Feinberg had drunk to break through the barrier and merge with her humanity, to create a new type of creature.

No one came and Sheila slid out the window, noticing that the crying human child was bleeding from its eyes.

Back at the warehouse, she set up her small laboratory. It was only as wide as a rafter but it had that essential ingredient without which all scientific research is hopeless. It had the trained mind of a scientist.

She worked quickly. She isolated the solution from the baby flesh. The rafter was just cool enough to keep it alive and surviving. Then she set up her human trap.

There was a pay phone in the office of the warehouse. She phoned an old acquaintance.

The acquaintance didn't recognize her voice but she was, oh, so susceptible to the bait.

"Look," said Sheila, "you don't know me. But I know you're pushing fifty . . . no, no . . . don't get mad. I've got something for you. I can take away your eye wrinkles. Yes. I know a lot of women in their thirties have eye wrinkles. I can take yours away. Of course it will cost money. Lots of money. But you don't pay me until I show you it works. You'll have skin like a baby's. Is it illegal? Illegal as hell."

Sheila surprised herself at her knowledge of human nature. She had never been able to be effectively deceitful before, possibly from having a mother more effective in information-gathering than the CIA. But now she had handled this woman perfectly. If she had offered the treatment free, the woman wouldn't believe it was worth anything. But when she said expensive and that was illegal, it was too great an attraction to resist. The woman was sure she could get baby skin.

Which was more than Dr. Feinberg was sure of. It had, however, a chance of working. That would lead to the second crucial step of her plan, formulated in the antique shop.

And if it didn't work?

Well, she was going to see the woman and at least she would get a meal.

The woman greeted her at the door of her fashionable Brookline house.

"I know you. You're that crazy Doctor Feinberg the police are looking for. You're a criminal. You're a deadly killer. You're a butcher."

40

"I can make you look ten years younger," said Sheila.

"Come in," said the woman.

She furtively guided Sheila into a study. The woman was nudging fifty with full hip and breast, well fatted and marbled throughout. Dr. Feinberg suppressed her hunger. The woman had dyed red hair. Very dry.

"How much money?" asked the woman.

"Lots," said Sheila. "But first let me prove what I can do."

"How do I know you won't poison me?"

"Do you think I would travel halfway across a city that is hunting me just to poison you? What's the matter with you? Who do you think you are? You think people stay up nights figuring out ways to harm you? Don't you think I've got better things to do?"

"I'm sorry."

"You should be."

Sheila took a capped test tube inside a water shield from her pocketbook.

"Drink this," she said.

"You first," said the woman.

"I don't have eye wrinkles."

"I don't trust you," said the woman.

"Do you trust your eyes?"

"Yes."

"Have they ever seen one wrinkle disappear from anybody yet? One? I mean really disappear. Not cosmetic surgery so that your face looks like drapery when the whole thing sags. New skin. I'm talking new, unwrinkled skin."

"I've got a lot of friends. I'll be missed immediately."

"I know that," said Sheila. "That's why I chose you. You're not going to be missed. We're going to use your friends."

"What if something should go wrong?" The woman

41

bit a perfectly formed fingernail. It was made of soft artificial lacquer, and it didn't bite well but rather stretched under her teeth.

"Then you still have your wrinkles. Hey, I'm giving you young looks, human."

The woman shrugged. "All of it?"

"Sure," said Sheila.

She uncapped the top.

"Quickly," said Sheila. "It's not that stable. All of it. Now." The woman hesitated. Sheila sprang to her and dumped the tube downward over the red tongue. She clamped the jaw shut with her powerful hands and closed the nose. Then she let the jaw open and the woman swallowed reflexively as she gulped air.

The woman made a face.

"Ooooh, that was awful. Let me wash it down with a drink or something."

"Don't," said Sheila. "It won't survive alcohol."

The woman blinked. She smiled. She collapsed on the white sag carpet and breathed slowly.

Sheila peered at the corner of the right eye. The eye was open and the pupil stared unseeing at the ceiling.

Two things would have to happen for this to work. One, Sheila's theory that each cell contained its own program and would, like a tumbler falling properly in a combination lock, go through the bloodstream to its right place. And two, speed.

Sheila herself was evidence that something happened quickly. Exactly what, she was not sure. But would specific changes happen quickly?

And was human saliva the key to keeping the foreign genetic material alive in a new body? She could only wait and see.

The woman's eyes were covered with some light oil. Sheila rubbed it with her thumb. If Sheila were correct, not only would there be the specific change— that is, the baby's cells in their proper relationship to the rest of the body, eye crease to eye crease, but—as with Sheila—a vast amount of changeover would occur almost instantly.

It may have been her imagination or great disappointment but the eyes suddenly seemed more wrinkled than before. Instead of a few lines, there was now a flutter of bumps like very thin paper veneer bubbled up with water. She heard the traffic outside honk for a light that lingered too long. She smelled the woman's light perfume. She touched the heavy crow's feet around the eye. The skin was dry.

Sheila sighed. She had failed. She wondered for a moment if her experiments in the lab had produced not a different species as she thought she was, but just another insane person. One who was so insane she liked human meat.

But if that were so, why was she so strong? How could she move so effortlessly? Perhaps it was the strength of a madwoman. She had heard of these things.

She rubbed the skin around the eyes between her fingers. It crumbled. Little cells giving up in dryness. And then she saw it. Skin removed left new skin underneath.

The eyelines were gone. At corners of the woman's eyes was smooth baby skin. The new cells had pushed out the old, making them even more wrinkly.

Sheila turned the woman's head. The other eye had a translucent white patch just where the eyelids met. With her fingertips, Sheila lifted it off and chewed it like a snack.

When the woman regained consciousness and saw her eyes, felt her skin, and turned this way and that to see how beautiful she looked from different angles—full face forward was best—she had one response as to what she would do for Dr. Sheila Feinberg.

"Anything."

"Good," said Sheila. "Now I know you have friends. And I want to help them too in a special way. I'm starting a special clinic."

"You'll be rich."

Sheila smiled. Rich was for humans. She wondered if her species would have a form of currency someday?

There were no thoughts about her species being a better species than man. Or worse. It didn't matter. Sheila Feinberg understood then, logically, what she had understood instinctively since the transformation, and what almost every soldier knows who has seen combat.

One kills not because one is right or brave or even angry. One kills to live. One kills others because they are others.

Despite all the reasons humans gave for wars, Sheila understood all those reasons were wrong. Humans fought not for justice or even conquest, but because they perceived another person as simply another person. A border. A language difficulty. Different clothes called uniforms. All made it easy to tell who were the others.

She had never studied political science or history as a student. But she knew she understood more about humans now than anyone who had ever majored in those supposed sciences.

Perhaps her species would be luckier and not fight among itself as humans did, but reserve its efforts for other species.

"Yes, rich," agreed Sheila. Let the human woman think she wanted money.

Sheila needed a young girl with big breasts, a young girl with a shapely nose, a young girl with flaxen yellow hair, a young girl with smooth and tender hips.

"Tender?"

"I mean smooth and full," said Sheila.

44

"That's quite an order for one girl."

"Oh, no. Different girls. But Caucasians."

"Your method only works with similar races?" the woman asked.

"On the contrary. There really isn't any difference between the races. It's a cosmetic thing. Who'd want to put a black breast on a white chest? Or vice versa?"

"How interesting," said the woman, not all that interested. She pulled up at the top of her left breast. She imagined what it would look like young again. She imagined what it would look like very big. She had always said she was glad she didn't have those big floppy breasts. She had always said big breasts were an American distortion, a cultural prejudice not shared by really civilized people.

"I know a 42-Double-D cup," said the woman, grinning. She imagined those battlements parading before her and felt quite excited.

Sheila had other problems. She hadn't eaten for a day. She fell on an old woman carrying a loaf of bread. Sheila left the bread.

The next day the young girls arrived.

Within twenty-four hours, Sheila Feinberg had the sort of features her mother had once called "gaudy."

The nose had lost its prolonging bump. The chest curved massively. The hips came out with soft invitation.

Her hair was long and golden blonde.

She could not be recognized by the police anymore, but even more important, with her new beauty, she now had an awesome power over the male human. Let the government send its best after her. First they would have to find and recognize her; then they would have to resist her physical charms.

Being searched for now wasn't the worst of her problems. She had to find a mate.

The day had become quite itchy for her. She restrained an urge to rub her back against door jambs and put her scent around greater Boston.

She was, quite simply, in heat.

She was ready to breed.

She had two more dinners and when the carcasses were found, bellies eaten out, agents from the federal government came pouring into the city. Secret Service men came, although the crime had nothing to do with the U.S. Treasury. FBI men, although the crime had nothing to do with federal laws. CIA scientists examined the corpses, although it was against the law for that agency to operate internally.

The mayor of the city, faced with a problem he neither understood nor had a remote chance of coping with, went on television to tell greater Boston:

"We have stepped up surveillance. We have increased our deployed forces and we are working toward what we expect to be a significant step in stemming this terror."

What he really meant was that the city, along with everyone else, was spending more money. Those who survived would be taxed more in the future.

It was summer and the humans of the city were preparing for their annual fall rioting based on color. But something in their midst knew more about them than they did. She knew all humans were alike.

She also knew that, counting the gestation period, the reproductive process might be too slow.

"Perhaps," thought Sheila," I can make others like me in a faster way."

And by others like her, she did not mean just big-bosomed blondes.

CHAPTER FOUR

Security around the Boston Graduate School of Biological Sciences, where the now notorious Dr. Sheila Feinberg had done her chromosome experiments, was typically tight.

Many men with many guns and serious faces annoyed passers by who wished to use the street in front of the lab. Men with long hair and beards were questioned. That there was no more reason to question men with long hair and beards than there was to question crew cut, well-dressed men didn't seem to faze any of the guards.

They did not know what they were looking for.

None of them knew what a chromosome was. One of the officers suspected it was vaguely left wing but was not sure. They had all seen pictures of Dr. Sheila Feinberg. Instead of a sexy, bosomy blonde, they were looking for a flat-chested woman with the whoop of a honker.

Remo and Chiun showed identification. It was a

standard little thing they used when they didn't want to invade a place. The identification showed they belonged to an intelligence branch of the agriculture department. Official enough to enter places, but not important enough to attract attention.

"That one's a foreigner," said a guard, pointing to Chiun.

"You're the foreigner," said Chiun. "You're all foreigners. But I am tolerant."

Chiun, once a strong lover of daytime television dramas, had once seen an episode on intolerance. He thought intolerance was wrong. He thought it was wicked. He vowed from that day forth he would try to make believe that whites and blacks were equal to yellows.

He had told this to Remo.

"From this day forth, I shall pretend your blood is as good as mine," Chiun had declared. "This is an act of tolerance and charity. I will tolerate all lesser peoples. This I have learned from your society."

"Little Father," Remo had said. "It is not the blood that makes one man better than another. It is what he has learned, what he has done, and what he thinks."

"And you have done so well, considering you were born white," said Chiun.

"You taught me because no one in your own village was worthy. You taught one of them once and he turned out to be a bummer. You had to go to the White world for a pupil. And you got me."

"I did not know you would learn so well. I taught more because you knew more. What you learned was why I taught. Not because you were white. I would no more go looking for a white to learn the secrets of Sinanju than I would seek an elephant to cut diamonds. However, you proved adequate and with my training techniques, lo, we have an elephant that cuts diamonds. Glory be to me."

"Is that one of your prayers or a waking-up exercise?" Remo asked. Chiun had not understood the insult but was sure it was more crabbing. When a gentle, loving blossom opens its most valuable blessings, it is done so that a nasty, little bee can stick unpleasantly into it. In this analogy, Chiun was the flower, Remo the bee.

The guard at Boston Biological squinted at the identification cards.

"You two are Remo Cloutier and Wango Ho Pang Koo. That right, Mr. Koo?"

"That is correct," said Chiun.

"Enter," said the guard.

On the way through, one of Chiun's fingernails snapped out with the whip coil of a snake's tongue. It was out and back before the guard noticed it.

The guard felt an itch on his wrist. When he rubbed it, his hand was bloodied. His wrist was bleeding. His ulnar artery had been severed.

This was not, of course, a random act of violence against the guard. Chiun regarded it as a gift to his employer.

Chiun, who had never seen any form of government like America's and was therefore dumfounded by Smith's reluctance to murder the president and assume the throne, understood that supposedly he and Remo were working for the American people. Remo had said the guard was an employee of the people.

Thus, at the entrance to Boston Biological, Chiun, Master of Sinanju, had made an American servant a bit more responsive to his employers and less surly to the public in general.

He also let him know in a small way that intolerance, especially from a lesser race, would not be tolerated by a Master of Sinanju in America.

He had not left a guard sinking to his knees calling desperately for help to stem the flow of blood. Actually, Chiun had just spread a bit of understanding in a nation that needed it so much.

49

Not that whites were totally hopeless. There were things, he knew, at which they were good. The mysteries of their laboratories was one such thing. For the last century and a half, Masters of Sinanju had been returning to the Korean village with tales of Western mysteries. At first, how men could talk into machines and be heard many miles away, later, how men could fly and how pictures could be seen on glass screens and how, without any mental preparation, merely by inserting a needle, a Western medicine man could put someone to sleep so he would feel no pain.

There were so many mysteries to the west, especially wanton women with painted faces. Chiun himself, as a young man, had asked his Master and teacher about Western women.

"No," his teacher had said. "It is not true their private part goes in a different direction, nor does it have needles in it to hurt you if you do not pay them for their services."

"Then what are they like?" Chiun had asked, for he was a young boy and quite susceptible to tales of mystery.

"They are like what they are like. The great mystery is life itself. All else is what you know or what you have overlooked."

"I like mystery better," Chiun had said.

"You are the most unruly pupil a Master had ever had."

This comment was often made to the young Chiun but he had never told his own pupil, Remo, about it. Let Remo think that he himself was the most unruly pupil in the history of the House of Sinanju.

The Western laboratory was a wonder to behold. Beautiful glass shaped like stiff, fat fingers. Bubbling, clear bowls. Lights that crinkled with the power of the universe.

"It's just a laboratory, Little Father."

"I want to see the mystery dematerializer. I have

heard about it. I have not had a chance, lo, these many years to see one. Yet your magicians in these magical buildings have had them many years. Many years."

"I don't know what you're talking about. We've got to find Dr. Feinberg's old lab and figure out what the hell it is we're looking for."

"We are looking for a Western magic woman. Truly a dangerous species. For the power of the West has never been in their ugly white bodies but in their magical machines."

"There's nothing ugly about a white body."

"You are right, Remo. Tolerance. I must show tolerance to the fat meat eaters. Death-paleness can be beautiful to others who suffer the same death-paleness."

There were guards at Dr. Feinberg's old laboratory. They accepted the passes.

"I love these places," said Chiun.

A dark-haired man in his middle forties sat morosely behind a desk in the far corner of the room. He wore eyeglasses and stared straight ahead.

When Remo started to introduce himself the man began a lifeless rendition of what he had obviously told questioner upon questioner. He did not look at Remo when he spoke.

"No," was his first word.

"No. There is no more material that can be used to make another of what Dr. Feinberg has become. No, we do not know what the process is that made her happen. No, we do not have similar experiments underway. No, I am not now nor have I ever been a member of the Communist party, Nazi party, Ku Klux Klan or any group that espouses hatred or plans to overthrow the United States government.

"No, I had no idea this would happen. No, I do not know where Dr. Feinberg may be, nor do I know her personal friends, nor do I know whether she belonged to any lunatic groups."

"Hello," said Remo.

"Oh," said the man. "You don't want to question me?"

"I do," said Remo. "But I have different questions."

"Yes, we do," said Chiun.

"What have you been doing here these last few days?" asked Remo.

"Answering questions," said the man.

"Where do you keep your magic dematerializers?" asked Chiun craftily.

"In a minute, Little Father," said Remo. "Let me ask my questions first." And then to the morose man in the white coat, "Anybody ask you for anything other than information?"

The man shook his head.

"And you've done nothing but answer questions?"

"Nothing for the lab. My private life is my private life."

"Tell me about it," said Remo.

"I don't have to."

Remo tweaked the man's ear. The man thought if Remo wanted to know things that much, he would tell him. He was a lab assistant. His girlfriend had asked for some supplies. The man stemmed the flow of blood at his ear with a towel.

"And is your girlfriend Sheila Feinberg?"

"Are you kidding? Feinberg was built like a slab of sheet rock to her shoulders, Mount Rushmore above the chin. She was so homely, I hear electric vibrators rejected her. She had a face like a prune made ugly."

"What do you make for your girlfriend?"

"Anything she wants. She's got a set on her that would make a Jesuit burn dictionaries."

"Like what?"

"Well, we call it insulator. It's a chemical compound like gelatin that retards temperature changes in anything it surrounds."

"I see," said Remo, who felt there was something here that wasn't as innocent as it sounded.

"Now to serious business," said Chiun. "Where do you keep your magical dematerializers?"

"Our what?"

"Your wondrous devices that go round and round and make things out of other things?"

The man shrugged.

Chiun noticed a container of milk on the man's desk. It sat near a ball of cellophane.

Chiun's long fingernails came out of his kimono. He opened the milk carton wider. He poured the milk into an empty bowl on one of the laboratory tables, then swirled his finger around in the milk.

Gradually the bottom of the glass bowl appeared to hold water, and the top cream.

"It does that by magic instead of by hand," Chiun said to the laboratory assistant.

"My God, you're a walking centrifuge," the man said, amazed.

"That's the word. Centrifuge. The great mystery of the centrifuge that, with a flick of a switch, can do what the hand does. We never understood back home how you do it."

"With your bare hands, you did what a centrifuge does. That's incredible. How can hands separate elements?"

"You just do it. Let the fingers do it. How does the centrifuge do it?"

"By laws of science."

"Genius of the West," exclaimed Chiun. And then he watched the man do it with that wondrous device. No, the man said, they did not give away their centrifuges.

Perhaps, suggested Chiun, they could barter for it.

"What could you give me?" the man asked.

"Perhaps there is someone plotting to take your position?" asked Chiun craftily.

"As a lab assistant? It hardly pays enough to eat on."

"Little Father," Remo whispered to Chiun. "You know it is tradition that the House of Sinanju will not serve two masters."

"Shhhh," said Chiun.

"What sort of answer is that?"

"Shhhh."

"You can't do it," Remo said.

Chiun looked at the centrifuge. You could put any liquid you wanted into it and most often take out two different colored liquids. Sometimes three.

It was, and this was most obvious to anyone with any sort of reasoning power, not being used at the time. By anyone. The lab assistant didn't need it. He was only a servant in this place. Servants were notorious for betraying their masters.

And most importantly, this Remo had to understand, the servant could not possibly have enemies important enough to interfere with Remo and Chiun's service to Emperor Smith. By that, Chiun meant, they could avenge any slight being done to this poor servant and walk out with the centrifuge right now.

What could beat that?

"Not betraying the tradition of Sinanju," said Remo.

Because Chiun knew Remo was right and because Remo had exposed that he was, at this moment, more true to Sinanju than Chiun himself, Chiun said he would forget the centrifuge. But not because of what Remo had said.

"Good," said Remo.

"I will forget the centrifuge because you couldn't possibly understand how I could accept it and still be one with tradition. You are not ready for that yet. You are still young Shiva, young Destroyer, young night tiger, and as a cub there is much you do not know."

"I know we're not supposed to be making hits for this guy when upstairs pays our freight."

"You know nothing," said Chiun. "And you have helped me. I will write my romance about a teacher who gives everything, everything to his pupil and in return is denied a crust of bread."

"Are you two guys really from Agriculture?" asked the lab assistant. "I mean it's just a centrifuge. You can buy one."

"I send all my money home to feed a starving village," said Chiun.

"Too bad," the lab assistant said.

"You feel no sense of sorrow for me?" Chiun asked.

"I got my own problems," said the lab assistant.

And so angered was Chiun that such a decent person as himself should suffer without sympathy, that when the lab assistant said he had his own problems, Chiun offered: "Have another," and delivered a double hernia to the brute. The man rolled on the floor in agony.

"I think we needed him," said Remo. "He's pretty useless now. He's going to have to go to the hospital now. We really could have used him. We needed him."

"It does not strike me as all that strange," said Chiun, "that you are most aware of your own needs when others' needs go unmet. Not strange at all."

The lab assistant's legs came up in fetal position. His hands gripped his groin. He made big weepy noises. Guards ran in. They had heard the sound.

"He fell," said Remo.

The guards saw the man in incredible pain. They looked at Remo and Chiun suspiciously.

"Very hard," said Chiun.

"He . . . he . . ." groaned the attendant, but could not finish his sentence because of the pain and did not have the strength to point to Chiun as the perpetrator.

Chiun, having suffered nothing but insensitivity at the hands of that man, turned away. There was no one who was going to force him to tolerate such behavior.

"That's two, Little Father," said Remo. "Come on."

By that, am I to assume that the guard outside was not discourteous and this vicious animal here was not insensitive?"

"You two. What happened?" asked a guard.

So as not to be disturbed by the guards, Remo spoke in what Korean he knew. He told Chiun the last link between the woman they looked for and this laboratory had not yet been broken.

Chiun asked how Remo knew.

Remo explained that just because they happened to be girlfriends of lab assistants, girls did not go around asking for scientific materials. And lab assistants didn't just give such things away. That was ridiculous.

"Not that ridiculous," Chiun answered, looking at the centrifuge.

"Take my word for it, ridiculous," said Remo in Korean.

"What are you two talking about?" asked the guard.

"Centrifuges," said Remo.

"Don't believe you," said the guard. "Let's see your identification again."

This time there was a close examination of the ID cards.

"Hey. These are ten years old," said the guard.

"Well, then, take my universal identification, accepted everywhere in the world without question," said Remo. He snapped back the two cards with his left hand and with his right patted two finger pads

56

into the temple above the guard's left ear. He went to sleep like a baby.

The other guard said that looked like really good identification to him. Super identification. Best identification he had seen anywhere from anyone. No wonder it was accepted everywhere in the world. Would the two gentlemen like anything from the labs?

"Since you offered," said Chiun.

By the evening news, announcers had brought the Chromosome Cannibal, as they were now calling Sheila Feinberg, to the top of the hour again.

Police believed, according to the announcers, that the Chromosome Cannibal had joined forces with a pair of accomplices.

"A thin white man and an elderly Oriental, using false identification police said was almost as good as the real thing, bluffed their way past tight security and stole a key scientific instrument from the lab of chromosome-crazed Dr. Sheila Feinberg.

"Police are not commenting tonight on what this new addition to the scientist's arsenal will mean to greater Boston but all residents are urged to stay off the streets after dark. Do not go out alone. Report any mysterious behavior to the following police number."

Remo turned off the television set. Chiun smiled.

"You know," said Chiun, "if you put strawberry preserves into this thing, the pits go right to the top, the sugar sauce stays in the middle and the pulp goes to the bottom."

Remo signaled for quiet. Already the centrifuge noise had attracted the attention of the one nurse who had to be told it was only a patient in excruciating pain before she lost interest and left them alone.

They were in a room next to the one where the lab assistant lay. He had undergone surgery for his hernia and was now resting. There were no police guards on his door. Remo waited to see if he had a visitor.

He heard footsteps move down the hall, steps so light he almost missed them. He looked out. The woman came with a fashionable, white, draped dress and an expensive, groomed look, as if she had just come from posing for a magazine advertisement selling dresses to housewives fifty pounds heavier than she.

Except for a couple of things. She was a bit too busty and the hair was a bit too golden. Remo put his ear to the wall and heard her talk to the lab assistant.

"I couldn't find it, darling. Where did you leave it? In the inner storeroom? Why there? Yes, of course I love you. Got to run now. Good-bye."

Remo heard her leave the hospital room. He heard her steps down the hallway, remarkably soft for a woman in high heels. Most clomped with sharp bangs of stiff leather on stiff floors.

Remo left the room.

She padded up the hallway, and waited for an elevator. Remo waited with her.

"Nice night," he said.

She smiled coldly.

He let out a bit more of the smooth charm he had, the cool rhythm so many women found deliriously stimulating. He smiled his sexiest smile and let his thin body relax slightly.

"Nights like these are too nice to spend in a hospital," he said.

She didn't answer. He went down in the elevator with her.

"What's your name?" he asked.

"Why? Are you afraid of riding four floors with a stranger?"

"I hoped you wouldn't be a stranger much longer," said Remo.

"Really?"

"Yes," said Remo.

"That's nice," said the busty blonde.

Outside in the Boston street it was hot. The smell of exhaust clogged breathing and the pavement felt like hostile rock underfoot. The groan of racing engines reminded Remo that Massachusetts was supposed to have the worst drivers in the nation and what many people believed were the most trigger-happy state police. The woman went to a car in the parking lot.

It was a dark station wagon. Remo followed her.

He touched her arm gently. She snarled.

"Look, sweetie. Don't get uptight. We can be friends or not be friends."

"Not be friends," said the woman.

She got in her car. Remo got in the other front seat.

"How did you do that? The door was locked," she said.

"I'm a magician," said Remo.

"Then make yourself disappear," she said.

"All right, lady, I have a job to do. I think you're a link to that loony cannibal lady who's been running around Boston."

"Why?" she asked. But her voice was suddenly low as if confidence had been drained out of it.

"I told you I'm a magician," Remo said. "Although it's not too tricky to figure out who the hell would need that gunk back in the lab."

"The insulating gel," she said.

"Yeah," said Remo.

"You know, you are cute."

"I know that," said Remo. "I've trained at it. Women sense it. But, you know, the depressing thing is, now that I've got it, it's no big deal. It's only when you don't have it you think it's a big deal. Try to break yourself away from my cuteness for a moment," he said sarcastically, "and get back to the gel."

"Does anyone else know about me and the insulating gel?"

"Why do you ask?"

"Because," she said. She gently put a hand on Remo's chest. Her nails kneaded themselves ever so slightly into the finely tuned body. Remo looked at the hands and saw what he wanted to see.

"How long have you had your change?" he asked.

"What?" hissed the woman.

"Your face doesn't match your hands," he said. "Your hands are in their thirties. Your face is twenty-two, maybe twenty-three. How long, lady? And where is Dr. Feinberg? We can do this nicely or we can do this not nicely."

"Dr. Feinberg? She's right here."

Then Remo realized he had fallen into a common trap Chiun had warned him about from the very beginning of his training. Eyes that do not see, ears that do not hear, and noses that do not smell. This had been the warning and what it meant was that most people neither saw, nor heard, nor smelled but only lazily remembered things. Thus, seeing something, they would not really be aware of it but treat it like one of many. An example was a hot dog. The first hot dog a child ate would be sniffed, touched, and examined. Thereafter, the child would bite without testing. Which was all right for people and children and hot dogs, but not for a trainee of Sinanju who was to be more alive than others.

Remo felt the mistake in his chest. The nails tore flesh and cut into bones. He had treated this person as a busty, young, blonde woman, as if she had spent more time with her hairdo than her pushups.

Which was obviously wrong. Remo let out a scream of pain as the hand raked across his face, gouging nail slits into his cheeks like someone ripping flesh with pliers. Worse, he had panicked. It was as if a buttercup had suddenly slashed at him with a stiletto.

In that instant, facing sudden death unprepared, it was as if Remo had never been trained. The panic made him throw a simple unbalanced punch that went harmlessly into the air.

He felt his stomach spill from his torn belly with another swipe from the hissing creature. It was like being locked in a blender helpless.

The panic had run its course. The pain was old. It was old because years of training had made it old. Degrees of suffering had been suffered in gymnasiums, on boats, in fields. When he thought his body could stand no more pain, when his early eating and sloth were pulverized within body and mind, he finally let out the greater rhythms of the universe.

Letting out man at his ultimate.

Now this ultimate man, born in America, but with a power of millenia within, forged within, trained within, so marrow-deep it was learned before he was born and in crucial times, cracked down to his essence as a man, and no longer remembered but lived. Now, in full force, bleeding from his belly, terror in his throat, and his own death before his eyes, Remo, adopted son of Chiun, Master of Sinanju, struck back for the human race.

The pain was too much.

The terror was too much.

But retreat was over.

Remo caught a bloody hand sweeping with animal power at his head. A cuff for a kill. But while the yellow-haired killer in the car fought by instinct, Remo fought as man. In his mind he slowed the blow, forcing himself to catch the woman's nails as they went to his head. His left hand caught the soft webbing of her hand between fingers and snapped down, making her thrust work against the drive of his hand.

So fast the human eye could not see it. First her hand out, then her hand an immobilized paw in pain.

And strike again did Remo. Fingers flicking into

her crazed eyes. Foot snapping into midsection. He felt her chestbone break. Hit again into the ribs. Driving ribs toward heart. Bleeding into already blood-washed seats.

The car rocked and a window pane went shattering onto the hot, sticky asphalt.

Blood coated the windshield like film on the inside of a strawberry malted glass.

The thing that was Dr. Sheila Feinberg screamed and hissed and moaned and could no longer stand the pain that man had withstood. She hobbled from the car.

Remo collapsed.

I guess I'm going to live, were his last thoughts. *But it hurts so much I don't want to.*

CHAPTER FIVE

Dr. Harold W. Smith had been organized since the age of three and a half. The last bit of untidiness in his life was in the second grade at Gilford Country Day School when someone spilled ink on his notebook. In those days, everyone used ink from inkwells.

Harold did not snitch.

Harold was not a snitcher. He was also not argumentative, although teachers did note a certain stubbornness in Harold when he thought he was right. He was not afraid of bullies, nor of the principal, whom he never failed to call "sir."

"Yes, sir, I do think you are wrong, sir." This during a full auditorium assembly with half his class giggling that Harold was "going to get it now, get it good."

Perhaps it was that principal who saw something worthwhile in the boy's courageous integrity. Smith never forgot how the principal said in front of everyone, and that included Betsy Ogden, "Yes, Harold,

63

you may be right. And I think we can all take a lesson from what you have shown us here today—standing up for what you believe is right."

Later, psychologists would call it reinforcement. But to the young Smith boy, it was like a medal he would never lose. Later, when his country had to select a man of impeccable courage, integrity, and incredible organizing skills to head such a potentially dangerous organization as CURE, they chose the man who had been that boy at Gilford Country Day School.

The cover for the great computer bank that linked and organized information was Folcroft Sanitarium in Rye, New York. So organized was Smith that the sanitarium business took him only fifteen minutes a day which meant his real business could get his normal, fourteen-hour work day. He worked six days a week and, if they came on some day other than Sunday, he took off a half day Christmas and a half day on July Fourth.

In the early years of the organization, he could get away to golf. But things had not gone well and the grooved swing he had learned in his twenties left him. As he got worse at the game, he wanted to play less. And there was less time to play.

So on this spring day a remembrance of green fairways came to Dr. Harold W. Smith as he sat in his office overlooking Long Island Sound through one-way windows. To his left was the computer terminal, the only one which gave unscrambled information from the CURE Computers and at his right, the telephone, connected to only one other phone in America. And that other phone was in the White House.

Smith waited for his line to ring. He would need this day all the integrity and courage he could muster.

He idly watched a printout of some information from the Chicago grain exhange. Some millionaire family was trying to corner the soybean market again. It looked so easy and incredibly profitable to these people who wanted to control one of the basic foodstuffs of the modern world, then push up prices. It always looked so easy and yet never worked.

It never worked because, as one of its side functions, CURE never let it work. This time the computer would order an agent in New York City to let information leak out about an attempt to corner the market. Other speculators would make the price just too high. Sometimes the families were reminded that their firms had done something illegal a few years back and, while the families themselves were not guilty, it certainly would be unpleasant for them to be indicted and stand trial. This usually came from a local district attorney.

Neither the agent who leaked the takeover rumor nor the district attorney who threatened the indictment would ever know for whom they really worked.

Only three knew.

One sat by a phone.

Another looked into the endless dark pit of death.

The third took time from a busy day to take a red telephone from a dresser drawer in his sleeping room.

The phone rang at Smith's desk.

"Yes, sir," he said.

"What's happening in Boston?" The voice was deeply Southern, but without warmth. This President talked softly but with the biting sting of sharpened steel.

"The person is on it."

"And that means?"

"As I have said. Our special person is on it. He will be more effective than the teams of men you originally wanted to send."

"I regret sending smaller units," the President said. "I regret sending only enough men from enough departments to make it seem as though we were handling things. I regret not letting my department heads handle it."

"Do you want me to pull him out?" Smith asked.

"No. What reports are you getting?"

"None."

"Weren't you supposed to hear from him today?" the President asked.

"Yes."

"Then why haven't you?"

"I don't know," Smith said.

"Do you mean that something has happened to him? That the doer of miracles has failed? Smith, I don't have to tell you that this is a national emergency. Right now it's contained in Boston, but when it stops being contained, not only is this country in danger but the whole world."

"I am aware of the dangers. It may not be that harm has befallen our special person."

"Then what?" asked the President.

"Sometimes he doesn't get the coding in the phone numbers correctly. Sometimes he forgets to call. Usually he just doesn't bother."

"In a national emergency?" The President's voice was horror-struck.

"Yes."

"And this is the man who is between the human race and possible extinction?"

"Yes."

"And the Oriental?"

"He doesn't believe in telephones," Smith said.

"And you consider these two satisfactory for the mission? Is that what you are telling me, Smith?"

"No, sir, I am not telling you that they are satisfactory."

"Then what in the pluperfect hell are you telling me?"

"I am telling you, Mr. President, that I have assumed for this organization the defense of the human

66

race. That is what we are dealing with, the defense of the species and nothing else. I am telling you I assumed this defense because I had at my disposal the two men who, in the entire history of our species, are the most capable of defending our species from another which might turn out to be stronger and wiser than we. There are none better than my two men, sir. None. I would have been remiss had I not ordered them to duty."

"Yet they don't report in," the President complained.

"Sir, they are not generals made by Presidents or Congresses. You do not pass a law to make a Master of Sinanju. Two hundred people running down every street in America, proclaiming someone a Master of Sinanju could no more make someone a Master of Sinanju than could repeal the law of gravity. A Master of Sinanju is the finest human killing instrument ever made. And it is made only by another Master of Sinanju. The best you have ever known, heard of or read about in your lifetime has been only a pale imitation of these two men."

"No, sir, they do not report," concluded Smith.

"From what I hear, they haven't even taken a look at the parents' house, which I think would be a natural place for Dr. Feinberg to go."

"Mr. President, that woman, or actually, female of the species, is no more related to her parents than you and I are related to baboons or any other species. That woman is a new species."

"Dr. Smith, I think you have mishandled this situation and, as are the conditions of your organization, I am thinking of dismantling you," the President said.

Smith's voice was chillingly metallic. "Sorry, sir. When we worked only for our country I would have shut down immediately upon word from any president. But that is not the case now. You cannot close us down now because we are working just as much for some herder in a yak tent in the Gobi Desert of Mongolia as we are for the American people."

"What if I order physical force against you?"

"Sir, a few thousand marines with perhaps ten years of training are hardly going to be a match against thousands of years of training of the Masters of Sinanju. Really, Mr. President, that is very silly. For all you know, they could have me hidden in your own White House right now. And I think you understand that as well as I."

"Yes, I do," the President said slowly. "I saw them in action once. All right. There is nothing I can do now except turn off this line. You are now disconnected from service because I will not call on you. One other thing, Smith."

"Yes, sir?"

"Good luck. Go with God."

"Thank you, Mr. President."

Harold Smith waited for the phone to ring again. He waited all day and when it became dark on that spit of sea water known as Long Island Sound, when his watch said 9:01, he knew the last time that day for Remo to call had passed.

He did not have forebodings about his two men because Harold W. Smith did not allow forebodings any more than he allowed hope.

Those who had put him in charge knew his strength was his rational power. Yet he could not now push away thoughts of Remo when he first came to Folcroft. How young he seemed then. He had a bright open face with just a little baby fat.

Stop it, Smith told himself. *He is not dead and you have no evidence that he is dead.*

Smith also told himself that Remo had become something other than just an enforcer arm, something so much different and so much better than the average person that one should feel no more affection for him than one would feel for the fastest airplane or the finest watch.

A few lights blinked in the Sound. They were boat lights in a vast darkness. Smith realized his lights were still off in the office. He had not turned them on when it had gotten dark.

He watched the lights of the Sound and after a while left his office and went home.

Good-bye, Remo, he said softly to himself as he was leaving. He did not know why he had that hunch.

In Boston, the assistant director of the local office of the Federal Bureau of Investigation saw orders come through to remove even more men from the Chromosome Cannibal Case. He started throwing in-files and out-files into the round wastebasket. He cabled Washington headquarters that he had already had too few agents on the matter and the case was being so scantily and ineptly covered that he wasn't sure they would ever find out with what they were dealing. If they did, they probably wouldn't be able to handle it anyway.

An answer came that he should carry on in the fine tradition of his office, within the parameters set down by Washington. Which in real language, the kind not used by the FBI, meant, "Go blow your nose. Leave it to the local cops to screw up. We're protecting our ass and you should do the same."

It was the Vietnam attitude brought home, the attitude where getting a job done properly was not nearly as important as protecting yourself. It was understandable when men could be indicted for doing their jobs in a way some legal stickler didn't like. After a few trials you had men not trying to protect the public, but themselves. If you were indicted for doing your job too vigorously, then you did your job so as not to be indicted.

It happened with local police forces. Changes were ballyhooed as measures to improve the legality of police forces, to make them more responsive to the citizenry. What happened was the police, after a few court cases, took to protecting themselves and now criminals had taken over the streets.

The American public had had it with a war they lost, with city streets they lost and now, with the FBI, they were losing their national security. The great disasters America had suffered never came as disasters but as improvements.

John Hallahan, assistant director of the Boston office of the FBI, vowed late that warm night he would not let his superiors get away with it.

Let them try to protect themselves when the story got out that the local office was being cut back, despite the threat to the city by the chromosome killer.

John Hallahan was forty-eight and knew how to protect himself. First, he tidied his office. Then he told four subordinates to make a report on the best way to deal with this menace, considering they were being cut back in manpower.

"Of course you realize how sensitive this whole matter is and I expect you to carry out your jobs with traditional Bureau excellence." There was a giggling snort from one.

No matter, Hallahan realized. He had just created his own defense screen. When everything exploded in the papers, there would be four others to share the blame. While he might be shipped off to the Bureau in Anchorage, Alaska, he would still collect his pension, still have his income, still have his benefits.

This small triumph of rebellion brought little joy to Hallahan. He remembered when there was pride in what he did, the kind of job that made even the preservation of your own life less important, the sort of work burden that made your life happy.

The joy of a successfully concluded case. Of nailing someone really tough to nail. Going head to head against the greatest spy system the world has ever known, the KGB of Russia.

FBI meant something then.

You worked sixty hours a week, often seven days a week. You weren't paid as much as now with the new regulations. The time was less, but oh, how long the weeks seemed now, when you just counted the days to your retirement. You weren't defending a country anymore. You were defending yourself. The country be damned.

What did he want to say to America? Stop hurting those who want to help you? Don't you know who your real friends are? When was the last time a bank robber ever did you any good? Or a terrorist?

Yet those were the very people so many in Washington seemed peculiarly hellbent upon defending. As if all you had to do was mug some old lady to show you had some great moral complaint against the only country that ever existed that gave so much to so many if they would just work for it.

The only country.

The night people came into the Boston office and James Hallahan left. He was off to turn on his own bureau. He had sworn an oath once, but that was a long time ago when oaths meant something. He realized that was when he was happy.

The Boston *Times* reporter was late. Hallahan had a beer and a shot of rye. He was a scotch on the rocks man now but he remembered his father drinking this drink and the boozy, old-wood atmosphere of the South Boston bar. When he had been accepted to Notre Dame, his father had bought him a beer here and lots of people bought rounds. He had gotten tipsy and everybody laughed. And of course, graduation. How his father had cried to think his son, James Hallahan, the son of a man who collected other people's

71

garbage was "now a graduate of Notre Dame University, the United States of America. Oh, the glory of it, son."

Someone down the bar had said universities in America weren't as good as universities in Dublin, couldn't hold a candle to them, as a matter of fact. Of course in this Irish-American bar, that started a fist fight. Then came the law degree from Boston College.

Of course another drink to celebrate. And James Hallahan's confession. "Dad, I'm not going to practice law. I'm going to be an agent for the FBI."

"A policeman?" his father asked, in a state of shock. "On your mother's grave, son. We broke our backs to make you something. Why, you could have been a policeman right out of high school. You didn't need all that educating. We could have gone right to Alderman Fitzpatrick. It wouldn't have cost a penny. It's not like we're Eyetalians what's got to pay for it and all."

At that the young Hallahan had laughed. He tried to explain to his father what the FBI was, but the senior Hallahan was not someone to whom one explained things. The senior Hallahan did the explaining. And his explanation was simple. The boy's dead mother and the boy's father had worked, had sweated and labored with great pride because they knew their son was going to be somebody.

Well, all right. Man owes what he does with his life only to God. The senior Hallahan was accepting whatever God's will was concerning his son. He wanted the whole saloon to know that.

If young Jimmy wanted to be a policeman, then, damn it, he'd be the best lawyer policeman ever.

Of course, there had been an added word driving home. "You know, Jimmy, it's like educating a son to be a priest and him going to the fine universities in Rome, then coming home and takin' some job in a shoe store, like. It's not that sellin' shoes don't have its virtues; it's that, why bother to get some big, fancy education if you're only going to be a public employee like your father?"

"Pop," said Jim Hallahan. "When you talk about yourself, it should never be 'only a public employee.' But you'll see. Being with the Bureau is important. I think more important than being a lawyer."

His father was asleep. Jim Hallahan carried him into the house, already then with a cancer that would kill him, already then lighter than before, but with no one knowing it.

Within the next year, his father found out what the FBI stood for because he bothered to listen. It was not with a little pride that he eventually told anyone he could corner that his son was with the Federal Bureau of Investigation, the best in the world. "You have to be a lawyer or an accountant to get in."

"Pride of the nation, they are," his father had said.

Then he went into the hospital for a stomach operation. They discovered the growths and stitched him back up. Within three months he was gone. The funeral mass was said at the same church in which he was married and Jim was baptized and confirmed and where he had gone so many times to ask God's will and blessing.

At the wake, in the house his sister, Mary Ellen, would later take over, her having the biggest family, one of his father's friends said, "He was the proudest of you, Jim. Of all of you, he never stopped talking about you and that FBI. You'd think it was made up of angels from heaven."

And at that Jim Hallahan cried, without knowing why. He didn't try to explain it. He excused himself and went into his parents' bedroom, to the bed they would never use again, the bed in which he was conceived, and buried his head and bawled with a painful joy that could only be described as glory on earth.

73

It was a long time ago.

It was when there was pride in the Bureau. So long ago when life and its heavier burdens were light . . . and now, just showing up in the morning at the Boston office was the second heaviest chore of the day. The first was getting up in the morning.

Hallahan ordered a double rye. To hell with the beer. He looked at his watch. The *Times* reporter was late. The double shot came and Hallahan lifted his glass. Then he felt a hand on his. It was Pam Westcott, looking a good twenty pounds lighter than usual. She had obviously walked with stealth because usually one could hear Ms. Westcott a half block away as she galumphed her telephone pole legs down the block.

"Hey, Pam," said Hallahan. "Losing that weight's taken twenty years off you. You look marvelous."

"You can't diet away eye wrinkles, Jim."

"Dry martini on the rocks," said Hallahan, ordering a drink for the reporter. Pam Westcott seemed to go on martinis and potato chips. A lunch without four drinks for Ms. Westcott was not lunch. Hallahan had heard from several public relations men that Ms. Westcott was probably an alcoholic but ate so much her weight problem would probably kill her heart before the booze smothered her liver. She was forty and used to look fifty. This evening she looked, positively, in her late twenties. There was an easy slowness to her. A stalking confidence. And she had no eye wrinkles.

"Nothing for me, Jim, thanks."

"Hold the martini," Hallahan said. "How about a couple of bags of potato chips?"

"Thanks, no."

"Wow, you *are* on a diet," Hallahan said.

"Sort of. High protein."

"Okay, how about a hamburger?"

Pam Westcott shook her tawny locks and looked up at the bartender.

"Make it four of them. And raw. And lots of juice."

"You mean blood, lady?" said the bartender.

"Yes, lots of it."

Hallahan lifted his drink again. He felt her strong hand on his.

"Stop," she said. "No more alcohol."

"Hey, Pam. You a reformed drunk?"

"Say I'm a reformed person, all right? Don't drink."

"I want a drink. I need a drink. I feel like a drink and I'm going to have a drink," Hallahan said.

"You're a fool."

"Hey, do you want the story I promised? Don't you want that?"

"Yes, but I want more."

"Okay," Hallahan said. "The deal is this. I give you the story. You give it to another reporter for his by-line so that when the story comes out, I have no trouble because I've never talked to that reporter. That's the deal."

"I've got a better one for you, Jimmy."

"Just so long as it doesn't stop me from having my drink."

"But it does," said Pam Westcott.

"You turning into a Baptist or something?"

"Hallahan, you know I'm a good reporter. Forget my girlish good looks."

Hallahan suppressed a smile. There had never been girlish or good looks about Pam Westcott. At least not until now.

"I want to show you something. Come to my place tonight. Let the booze go out of your system. I'm going to give you something you'll thank me for forever."

"I'm married, Pam."

"Jeezus. C'mon, Jim."

"I'm pretty down. I want the drink, Pam."

75

"Give me four hours."

"I'm tired, Pam. I don't have four hours."

"How many drinks have you had so far?"

"Two. And a beer."

"Okay. Two and a half hours. I'll give you the biggest case of your life. You'll retire with more benefits than you can shake a subpoena at."

He wanted the drink but told himself if this reporter wanted him not to drink so much and promised so much, why not give it a shot?

The bartender dumped a plate of four raw hamburgers on the bar. Heads turned. He emptied a small plastic bowl on top of the pile of hamburgers. Red beef blood poured out. More heads craned.

Pam Westcott smiled at all the pale, boozy faces and, careful not to let it spill, lifted the plate. Then the reporter from the Boston *Times* tilted the plate, drank the blood and, in a few healthy bites, finished the hamburger and licked the plate clean.

A drunk at the end of the bar asked if she cared to do the same to his meat someday. There was laughter, the kind of laughter men let out when they do not understand something but will not admit they are somewhat uneasy. Besides, one had to laugh at sexual jokes or someone might think one effeminate.

Pam Westcott lived just off Beacon Hill. She told Hallahan she couldn't divulge what she had discovered until all the alcohol was out of his system.

Well, then, could he have a bite to eat? Some potato chips? She didn't have any in the house.

"You without potato chips?"

"I don't like them anymore."

"I can't believe it."

"Believe it, Hallahan, believe it. I'm going to show you a lot more than potato chips."

"Aren't you interested in these chromosome killings? I've got a hot, juicy leak for you. We're abandoning this city to the man-eater. The order came

76

today just when two more people were killed at opposite ends of the city. Almost at the same time. This thing can move around with incredible speed."

"You'll see," said Pam.

What she had wanted him to wait for was another drink. Hallahan wanted to know what was in it.

"A vitamin," she said.

"I'm not drinking that," he said. It looked like whipped brownish gelatin. She had brought it to him in a very old shrimp cocktail jar, the kind that comes prepacked with heavy sauce and miniscule shrimp. The jars were often used afterward as drinking glasses. She had taken the jar out of a stainless steel box set on the kitchen counter. The box was plugged into a wall socket.

"I wouldn't drink that with a gun at my head," said Hallahan.

"I didn't think you would."

"You're damned right I won't. That stuff is funnier-looking than a cyanide cocktail."

Pam Westcott smiled. Then she leveled Hallahan onto the couch. Rape, he thought. Of course, that would be impossible considering his feelings toward Pam Westcott. It was impossible for a woman to rape a man who wasn't properly aroused. Especially Jim Hallahan, who hadn't been properly aroused since he saw the doctor's bill for his last child.

He pushed at her with just enough force to move her away. But she didn't move. He pushed harder at Ms. Westcott. She held him with one arm.

All right, Hallahan thought. *I'm pushing fifty and not in the best shape of my life, but I can sure push away a Boston* Times *reporter. Especially one holding me with one hand and a shrimp cocktail glass with the other.*

The holding arm got a hand around to squeeze his nose. He couldn't breathe. This woman was holding him with ease. He tried punching. His hands were pinned. He brought a knee up into her groin. This was a fight for life. The knee struck but she only growled.

Jim Hallahan opened his mouth for a desperate breath of air. In came the brownish goo. It tasted like liver left out for a day in the sun, then blended with butterscotch pudding. He retched but his mouth was clamped shut. He swallowed his own vomit.

His head moved as if someone was spinning it at the end of a long rope. The rope got longer and longer and longer and his head was at the end of it.

He was in a dark place and heard his father's voice begging him not to leave, then it was his mother's voice and then like a dream of going out from darkness to light that hurt his eyes. His eyes hurt terribly. Someone was shining great lights into his eyes.

"Turn off the lights," he said. He was thirsty and hungry. There was nothing in his belly to quench the hunger. Pam Westcott sat next to him purring. He smelled her. She smelled reassuring and safe. His own clothes, on the contrary, smelled bad. Smelled different. Somehow they made him very hungry.

"Do you have anything to eat?" he asked.

"Would you like a martini?"

The idea made Hallahan turn up his nose. He stretched. He yawned. Pam Westcott licked his face.

"I have something I know you'll like. Be back in a minute, kitten." Hallahan sat up with a slow ease. Hungry, yes. But also more alive. He realized that he had thought about the Bureau almost every moment since he had joined. He noticed the most startling fact of his life, that at that moment, he didn't care about the FBI at all, and he felt very good about it.

It didn't matter whether he turned on the FBI or not. It didn't matter whether he rose to the top of the organization or not.

Food mattered. Safety mattered. Reproducing mattered, provided he got the right scent.

He smelled it before he saw it, but knew the smell. It was a heaping delicious bowl of lamb intestines dripping in its own tasty blood.

He devoured it and licked himself clean. When he was finished, he saw Pam Westcott smiling at him. He smelled something very stimulating and when she turned her back he knew what would be wanted and taken.

They went into the bedroom, however, as if they were humans.

In the days that followed, he remembered an old joke about how if you were black on a Saturday night you'd never want to be white again. Well, this was like Saturday night every night and every morning. There were needs; they were met; and then there were more needs.

The biggest difference was that there was no worry. You felt hostile at times. Every now and then when you sensed a flame you felt frightened. But you did not carry fear over in your imagination and let it lead to worry.

Death was death. Life was life. Eating was eating. When he saw his family the night after he had stayed with Pam Westcott, he didn't want to stay at home anymore. He saw his youngest son cry and what seemed strangest of all he didn't care as much as when he used to see a hurt animal. There was nothing.

Moreover, he couldn't understand why his son was so upset. His mother would provide food and shelter. What was this boy doing tugging at his sleeve? Jim Hallahan cuffed him and sent the tyke tumbling across the room.

Then he stalked out of his house and went to the office. He started work with salivating gusto. He had something to look for. A wounded Caucasian with a torn belly.

Every hospital had to be checked. Every doctor

had to be checked. This was his order to his subordinates. He wanted that man, a young white man, with dark hair and eyes, and very thick wrists.

"Sir, what's the crime he committed?"

"Just do what you're told," said Hallahan. It was hard sitting with these men now. But Pam had taught him a trick. When things got very hard, eat bloody hamburger or steak, beef liver or kidneys. That would hold the hunger for the flesh of men. There was nothing to worry about because soon there would be all the flesh he would want.

Jim Hallahan knew this would be so. For now he had a leader far more powerful than even J. Edgar Hoover used to be.

Her name was Sheila, and she wanted that white man alive.

"He's wounded and probably been admitted to the hospital in the last two days?" Hallahan said.

"Yes," Sheila Feinberg had said.

"That's not the best of leads," said one of Hallahan's men.

"Drop everything else and find that man," said Hallahan.

"Yes, sir. Is there something wrong with my tie?"

"No," said Hallahan, opening a drawer in which raw liver was kept. "All of you get out now."

Outside his office one of his men asked the others, "Did he growl? Or was that my imagination?"

CHAPTER SIX

Mrs. Tumulty had a whale of a story. She wasn't going to gossip it away over some fence in the South End to amuse Mrs. Grogan or Mrs. Flaherty. She was on her way to the North End.

If Boston was an American melting pot, it was as melted as Europe with boundaries between different groups. There were the Irish in the South End, Italians in the North End, Blacks in Roxbury and only court orders for busing made any of them mix, and then only unwillingly.

Mrs. Tumulty strode purposefully through the streets of the North End with its strange-smelling foods and long names that ended in vowels. Her imagination had people behind glass windows of shops secretly doing all sorts of sex acts. She imagined stilettos in people's purses and jackets.

She saw people talking with their hands. "Except for their names," Mrs. Tumulty contended, "you can't tell the Eyetalians from the Jews and, after all, who would want to?"

To Mrs. Tumulty the country was filled with too many un-Americans. These included Yankee Protestant families who weren't really American enough.

She had some complaints about her church too. Too many Eyetalians. She always thought of them as sort of imitation priests, not the real thing. To Mrs. Tumulty, tolerance and intergroup understanding meant talking to people whose parents came from Cork or Mayo, different counties in Ireland, no matter how painful it was, people whose parents, you knew, kept chickens in the kitchen.

When the big scare about the man-eaters began, with all the talk about changing the basic nature of the human body through chromosome action or something like that, Mrs. Tumulty knew the television people were only covering up.

Foreigners always acted like that. Wasn't she telling you all the time? Foreigners with bumpy noses. Dark foreigners. Even yellow-haired Swedes. The most degenerate people on the face of the earth.

There was one strong, abiding lure that drew Mrs. Tumulty from the bosom of the decent people of South End into foreign quarters. Word had it there was a lot of money around for certain information.

This thing called the "word" was the only thing in Boston that moved freely among groups. Word had it if you knew of someone's special safe, discarded somewhere after a burglary, there was money for it. Word was that any late model pink Lincoln Continental would bring $5,000 or that the whereabouts of someone who had stiffed his neighborhood loan shark could get you $500.

Word in Boston was a tribal drum connecting many different tribes that made up the city.

Word in Boston that day was there was an awful lot of money for a wounded man, a cut-up man, a man cut up badly, almost like the victims from the human animal killer, Dr. Sheila Feinberg, another foreigner.

And about the cut-up man, Mrs. Tumulty knew. Just the other day, a skinny old Chinaman dragged up a bloody young man. He did it in a strange manner. The old Chinaman looked as if he couldn't lift a large potato, but was carrying this larger man like a baby with head over his shoulder and his right hand under the man's backside. The man was moaning. The old Chinaman wore a funny robe and said he saw an apartment-for-rent sign on the door of Mrs. Tumulty's house.

Mrs. Tumulty said she wished no trouble, but the old Chinaman with a white beard scarcely made up of a dozen strands pushed his way through easily.

Of course, there was money and paid in advance too, but then the smelly herbs came. She complained about that.

Here was the strangest part. The man was near death when the foreigner brought him in. By that evening, he was mumbling. By the next morning, his eyes were open. And his skin was healing a lot faster than normal skin.

What sort of black arts were being practiced, Mrs. Tumulty wanted to know. But she didn't press the point. Her boarders in the attic apartment paid well.

However, there had been a powerful stink coming from the rooms. She insisted it would cost more to clean things like the draperies to rid them of the smell. Every time she went to the attic, she tried to see more but the old Chinaman always managed to block her path. There were pots bubbling in there. She knew something really strange occurred because she saw the neck. It was a bloody mess when the Chinaman carried the bigger man, like a sleeping baby, up the steps. When she got a peek at that neck two days later, it was like an old burn. Mrs. Tumulty knew that wounds did not heal like that.

So she listened. From the beginning she listened because who knew what was going on, what with perversity and other sex practices abounding and all that? For a while, he talked in the funny Chinaman's talk, but then used common, decent, civilized English. She heard him telling the man his heart should do this, his spleen should do that and his liver should do this other thing—as though a person could make his body parts do different things.

And one thing he kept repeating.

"Pain never kills. It is a sign of life."

Which was mighty peculiar. But when the man answered back, the Chinaman talked Chinaman talk.

Now was the wounded man the one that word in Boston said was valuable to people?

This question did Beatrice Mary-Ellen Tumulty pose to the foreigner with the little, black, foreign mustache. He was the man she had come into this godforsaken Eyetalian section to see. Kept her purse over her lap all the time too.

Who knew what sexual insanity would overtake these men, their own women getting fat and mustached over twenty-one and all that. Mrs. Tumulty was fifty-three and a bit let out at the seams, she knew, but she had once been a looker and she still had those basic looks.

"Mrs. Tumulty," said the man she had come to the North End to see, "you have done yourself a good service today. I think that is the man who has caused so much trouble to the community. We know and trust you will keep these matters to yourself."

He took a large roll of fresh bills from his pocket. They were twenty-dollar bills. *Saints and glory,* thought Mrs. Tumulty. The man peeled off one and Mrs. Tumulty's eyes widened as he kept peeling. Two, three, four, five. The bills came fresh and new, down on top of one another, as the hand went back to the roll and came back with another bill. Six, seven, eight, nine, ten. Would the man never stop? It was delicious.

It drove Mrs. Tumulty to passionate fury. When twenty crisp new bills lay on the table in front of her, she let out a squeal of delight.

"You'll do a small favor now, please?" said the man.

"Anything," said Mrs. Tumulty, delightfully spent as the fresh strong bills went into her purse.

"Please go to this address," he said. "You will meet James Hallahan of the Federal Bureau of Investigation. You will get into no trouble. Just tell him what you have told me."

"Absolutely," she said and, in a sudden burst of gratitude, jumped from her chair and kissed the man's hand as she had heard Eyetalians did, don't you know? Just like he was a cardinal of the church or something.

But this man, she realized, was like a cardinal to his people. A leader of his community. A respected person and all she was doing was paying proper tribute.

Men wrestled Mrs. Tumulty away from her adoration of the man's hand. As she left the room, she swore eternal loyalty.

Thus did she meet, that afternoon, Salvatore (The Gas) Gasciano, who not only earned his nickname by the sound of his last name but because he liked to correct injustices and settle disputes with gasoline. He poured it and lit it. Sometimes on buildings and sometimes on uncooperative people.

But that had been in his youth. Rarely now had he set a match to anyone or poured gasoline into a car. He was a man of reason now. A man of respect.

He phoned the local office of the FBI. He got James Hallahan. He knew the lines were bugged. Every FBI office was bugged, his informants had told him. Besides, a man of caution would assume those people kept voice records.

"All right," were the first words spoken by Sal Gasciano. "We got your man. Now will you lay off a little?"

"You sure he's our man?"

"There's a lady coming up to see you. I don't know how many guys in Boston had their throats and bellies ripped last week, but this guy was torn up bad, Hallahan. So stop getting in the way of our business, okay?"

"If he's the one, we will. But I want one more thing."

"Jeezus, Hallahan, what the hell is the matter with you nowadays? We been staying clean on Federal things. Now you're all over us all the time. C'mon, Jim. Enough is enough."

"One more thing. A small thing."

"What?" asked Gasi Gasciano.

"You know Tony Fats?"

"Of course I know Tony Fats. Who doesn't know Tony Fats?"

"There's a large backyard behind Alfred Street in Jamaica Plains. Have him there at four o'clock this morning."

"Four A.M.? Tony Fats?"

"Right. The well-marbled one," came the voice of Jim Hallahan.

"All right, but Tony Fats doesn't know nothing. He just does small things. He's not even connected with people."

"Send him anyway."

"All right," said Gasciano. He hung up and shrugged. Marbled? Wasn't that what you said about good steak? But what difference did it make? The whole world was going crazy. Just so long as the North End remained the same. The same and sane.

Everybody else is crazy. One day, the Feds want

everything about some Jewish lady doctor they think is eating people. The next day they don't want to know nothing. Why, he had personally phoned to tell Hallahan to stop looking for one person and start looking for at least four or five. These crazy hits where bellies were eaten out had to be made by several people. They were happening too far in distance and too close in time. His estimate was four or five people, at least.

And what did that crazy Fed say? Jeezus, the guy didn't want to hear another word about it. One day, he wanted everything. The next day, nothing. Then, look for some guy whose throat was ripped. Then Tony Fats at 4:00 A.M. in Jamaica Plains. You'd think the son of a bitch was ordering dinner.

"We do so much work for the Federal government, we ought to get paid," said Sal Gasciano but didn't think it was all that funny.

When Mrs. Tumulty met the man in the car, she felt safe. It was a sedate, decent, black car and who, after all, was driving, but a man named Hallahan. Wouldn't you know? His mother had come from Kerry, the finest county in all Ireland, although his father did have a bit of Cork in him. But, you couldn't expect everything.

Wouldn't you know? He had worked for the FBI for many years, and risen to a position of prominence, which showed that even the godless Protestants who ran the country couldn't keep a good Kerry man down.

"We're not going to FBI headquarters."

"Darlin', wherever you wish to go is all right with me. I feel safe with the son of a Kerry woman. Oh, you don't know what's happening to Boston with all them foreigners and everything. Even have two at my house. One a Chinaman. But I rent to him. Take his money. He'd do the same to me and worse if I was in China, right?"

"Of course," said Jim Hallahan. He smelled the richness of fat sweat pores in salty gravy. He found out her home address and had her explain everything about the upstairs apartment, where the windows were, where the bed on which the wounded man lay was, and what were the buildings like that surrounded her own. And just how nosy were the neighbors?

"As nosy as a bunch of Mayo people," she said, referring to a county not quite as decent as County Kerry.

The good lad did not take her to FBI headquarters. Rather to an old warehouse, which, even on this fine day, was a bit drafty. She shivered a bit and got goose bumps. Was he really licking his lips or did he have a cold sore?

There were people in the warehouse who didn't look at all Federal. She felt like an early Christian being thrown into some Roman arena, what with everyone watching. These other people must have sores on their lips, too.

The warehouse had a funny odor. It smelled like barns that Mrs. Tumulty remembered from Kerry. She looked to Hallahan for reassurance. He was talking to a blonde woman with exorbitant breasts, clad in a tight black and yellow dress that was so shameful only a Jewess would wear one. The woman had suffered an accident apparently because the right side of her face was bandaged.

Mrs. Tumulty listened to the low murmurings of the people circling her. She felt better when she heard the topic. How could people discussing lunch be harmful?

"What's Hallahan brought for lunch?" said one.

"Looks like Irish stew," said another.

"Better than the Kosher food we had last night."

"I like French. There's a certain delicacy to French."

"Only after a bath."

88

"Which means twice a year you can have French."
"Give me dark meat any day."
"It's no richer than white meat."
"Nothing can beat a fine breast of WASP."

Mrs. Tumulty smiled. She had never heard of wasp breast but was sure it was something in melted butter without garlic or any of those other foreign spices that made you into a sex maniac if you ate them regularly.

She saw the agent Hallahan bow to the overly endowed woman in a peculiar manner. The head lowered, just as in a normal bow, but then came up to expose his neck.

A strange thing, she thought, for a Kerry lad with fine light-blue eyes, a rugged, dark, Irish face and a nose that showed by its crook its owner was not afraid of a manly fist.

He came toward her and the others closed around. Mrs. Tumulty was sure they were disguised agents because the ones she had seen on television and after a bank had been robbed by Africans, all wore very shiny shoes, neat suits, and tan raincoats. The agents in real life dressed just like on television.

The Kerry lad put a hand on her shoulder. The Kerry lad smiled. Mrs. Tumulty smiled. The Kerry lad lowered his head. Saints preserve us, what was he doing?

Mrs. Tumulty felt him put his manly lips to her chestbone. Not a Kerry lad, she thought. Not really. Some foreign molester in disguise. But suddenly there was a great ripping pain in her chest. It took her very knees away. It wrenched out her breath.

She was being dismembered and it was like she was an observer. She felt as if she was going down a great dark hole, deeper and darker than any hole she had ever seen. It was like the darkness from which she had come a long, long time ago. Her mother's voice was saying hello and that she should come along and not be late.

In the hole was a dream. She dreamed she was leaving her body. There was the Kerry lad over her body, his face bloodied, and all the other people eating away at her old tired body, their faces bloodied like cannibals.

And there was the yellow-haired woman limping over to join them.

Mrs. Tumulty was going home to her mother.

"Will there be only Kerry people?" she asked her mother.

"No, dear. There will be every kind."

"Good," said Mrs. Tumulty in her great dream. For now, just as the flesh back there did not matter, neither did the origin of the good people she would meet. They would be good people. Nothing else mattered anymore.

When the good parts of the body were eaten to bone, and the bones licked, the remainder, ligament and tendon, sponged into a green garbage bag and everyone licking their faces, Sheila Feinberg spoke to her pack.

"Jim has found the man I want. I will bear that man's child and make our species greater by the inbreeding. That man is the best of their species, stronger even than we are. Jim has found him. But it will not be easy to capture him."

"Will we get him for eating? You know, like after you've gotten his seed?" This from an accountant with a large insurance firm who was chewing on a fingernail. It was not his own.

"Possibly," said Sheila. "But he is the best of mankind; just capturing him will be difficult enough."

Hallahan had a thought. "Maybe he isn't just a man. Maybe, in other experiments like yours, he was created."

Sheila shook her head.

90

"No," she said. "I am aware of what is being done. This has never been done."

"Perhaps another country," said Hallahan. "Perhaps the Communists did it and that man escaped."

"No. We are the only ones."

For a moment in the warehouse there was sadness. It was not a soul-wrenching moment, but was like an echo of things that would never be again. It was very quiet.

"Hey, everybody," said Hallahan. "Four A.M. in the lot behind Alfred Street, I've got an Italian dinner set up. His name is Tony Fats and he's well-marbled."

There was laughter and Sheila said that four A.M. might be the right time to try to capture the human.

"What about the Chinaman?" asked the accountant.

This prompted another joke about whether he was Cantonese or Szechuan, these being kinds of Chinese cooking. But Sheila, who had been this new species longer than anyone else, felt that twinge of instinct, that touch of an animal's strongest emotion.

The emotion was fear.

Instinct told Sheila that man, with tender skin and weak muscles, upright man who was slow, who lived in packs and built things to protect his frailness, had not dominated the world by accident, but by superiority.

Yes, Sheila and her pack could fall on a single person but hadn't single persons always been vulnerable to most animals? Weren't human females always weaker? Children too until a decade and a half. Then, over forty, the human lost most of what little strength it had.

Yet humans ruled the world and animals lived in cages for humans' viewing pleasure.

No, there was danger in the old man. It would not be as easy as Hallahan thought.

For some reason, which Sheila attributed to inheriting the instinct of the man-eater, she feared the frail,

91

old Oriental more than the younger man. According to Hallahan, the Tumulty woman had said he was very old. Yet he had carried the young one upstairs easily.

When she thought of this old man, fear came as though there were loud drumbeats in the distance and a great noise far off.

She had not had dreams since the change. But in the warehouse where everyone waited before their hunt in Mrs. Tumulty's apartment, she had a dream while awake.

It was like an hallucination. It had smells and sounds. There, at the end of a long, long valley, was a little man who looked like a good meal.

But he wasn't. He was quieter than men they had taken. He was the very best of men, sent by the species to finish off Sheila and her pack.

Chinese food? Not at all.

She hoped that her pack would be able to save one of them—the young one or the old Oriental—for breeding. But maybe they wouldn't have that luxury.

In the attic apartment of Mrs. Tumulty's house, Chiun slapped at Remo's hand. Night was falling and, for the past three nights, Chiun had prepared the room.

"Don't pick at your wounds," Chiun said.

"That means not picking anywhere. I'm cut up bad."

"A scratch. It hurts because you heal. Death has no pain, but living does."

Chiun slapped the hand again.

"I'm scratching an itch."

"Disgusting," said Chiun. "Shameful."

Remo knew Chiun was not talking about scratching at wounds. Since he could formulate ideas and correctly interpret sounds and words, for seven hours now, Remo had heard Chiun over and over again tell him how disgraceful it was for someone representing Sinanju to get himself cut up this way.

As Chiun explained it, he didn't know why he was going to so much trouble to nurse Remo back to health.

"So that you can go out and embarrass me again? Do you know you almost allowed yourself to be killed? Do you know that? We have not lost a Master in 875 years. Do you not care what you do to my reputation?"

Remo had tried to protest that he had met something new but Chiun would hear none of it.

"You would get yourself killed? That is what you would do to me. And why? I will tell you why . . ."

"But, Little Father," Remo had protested.

"Quiet," Chiun had said. "You would do this against me because of my easy-going nature. I willingly gave up the centrifuge I was going to bring home to Sinanju as a part of a white man's magic display. Because I gave this up and was willing to do it, you sensed you could be killed against me. Who would care? Let the sweet, generous, loving, decent, fool Chiun go down in history as one who had lost a pupil."

"But . . ."

"I have been too generous. I have been too decent. I have been too giving. This is what I get in return. Carelessness with what I have made. Yes and why? Why? Because I am so generous. I am what you call a pushover. Yes, a pushover. Easy Chiun. Sweet Chiun. Agreeable Chiun. Come, world, take advantage of one who is too nice."

With that Chiun slapped a scratching hand and was silent. Remo knew Chiun became angry only after Remo could talk and reason. He remembered loving, soothing words in that dreamlike state while he was being treated by herbs and perhaps the most skilled hands available to kill or cure.

What most Western doctors did not know, and what Sinanju did, was that it was not so much a wound that killed, but the suddenness of it, or the fact there were many wounds. The human body was self-repairing. A single disease or injury to a single organ could be contained or eliminated by the body if the body had enough time to react.

A knife going into the brain kills. Yet, if it took a year to enter the human brain, the brain would form around it, accept it, try to reject it or do any one of many things to adjust to the assault. But, if the magnificent human body had to deal with it quickly, it could not adjust. Nor could the body deal with two assaults at the same time. That is why so many autopsies found what Sinanju had always known: that to die humans must suffer multiple wounds or diseases in more than one organ.

That knowledge was the basis of Sinanju's cures. The technique was to simply allow the body to fight one wound at a time. Every herb and massage worked toward this end.

Chiun with Remo's occasionally conscious help, treated first one injury, then another.

The great secret of all human healing was that humans did not heal; their bodies did. What successful drugs and surgery did was enable the human body to do what it was designed to do, cure itself.

With its nervous system refined through years of training. Remo's body did this better than all others on earth, with the exception of Chiun, the reigning Master of Sinanju.

And so Remo lived. But there was danger for night was coming. Remo wondered why Chiun was making special preparations.

CHAPTER SEVEN

Tony Fats got a reprieve because Sheila Feinberg and her tiger people, at four in the morning, came for Remo and Chiun instead.

The decaying residential street in Boston's South End was deathly still and had been for an hour as Sheila and her pack prowled noiselessly around Mrs. Tumulty's house. The circle had grown smaller and tighter with every full circuit of the old frame building.

In the attic apartment, Remo watched Chiun make elaborate preparations. The wizened Oriental ripped the wooden bottom from a kitchen chair and carefully hacked it with his hand into four lath-sized slats. Then he drove a steak knife through the center of each slat, and with rope mounted one in the frame of each of the small apartment's four windows. The tip of the knife pressed against the glass.

In the hall, around the apartment door, Chiun

sprinkled the contents of a four-ounce box of black pepper.

Remo rolled back and sank his head deep into the pillow.

"Very interesting," he said. "But why don't we just run?"

"Run and we run right into them. If they attack first, then we know the direction they come from and the direction we may escape in," Chiun said.

"A lot of trouble for somebody you say doesn't amount to much," Remo said. "You better hope they come. Otherwise you're going to have one helluva time explaining this mess to Mrs. Gilhoolihan or whatever that old harp's name is."

"They will come," Chiun said. He sat in a straight-backed chair next to Remo's bed. "They are out there now. Don't you hear them?"

Remo shook his head.

"How slow you are to heal. How quick you are to lose tone and technique. They are there. They have been there for the last hour and they will attack soon."

He reached out a long-nailed hand and pressed it gently against Remo's throat. Western doctors called it taking the pulse; Chiun called it listening to the clock of life. Then he shook his head too.

"We will wait for them."

Remo closed his eyes. He understood for the first time. If Chiun simply wanted to leave, he could leave anytime. But he feared he could not get through the tigers of Sheila Feinberg with Remo as excess baggage. So he was staying with Remo, conceding to the tiger people the opening attack, risking his own life by using a second-best maneuver he hoped would enable him and Remo to get out. Together.

Survival was the essence of the art of Sinanju but, to be done artfully, it had to be done single-mindedly. Survival was always more difficult when you were carrying a suitcase. If a battle were to come, Remo would be no more help to Chiun than a suitcase.

Suddenly Remo wanted a cigarette, really wanted one. It was not just the impulsive remembrance of a long-dead habit, but a desire that pinched at the inside of his mouth. He shook his head to drive the urge away and reached out a hand to touch the back of Chiun's hand.

The old man looked at him.

"Thanks," Remo said.

Not many words were necessary between the only two living Masters of Sinanju. Chiun said "Do not get maudlin. No matter what the legend says, these night tigers will find out they are not prowling around in the sheep fold."

Remo squinted. "Legend? What legend?"

"Some other time," said Chiun. "Stop your jabbering for now. They draw near."

In the street below, Dr. Sheila Feinberg, B.S., M.S., Ph. D., rubbed the back of her left ear and gave final instructions in a whispered feline voice.

"Save the young one for breeding. If the old one falls, do not eat him here. I think there may be more trouble if his body is found. Do not eat him here. But I want the young one saved."

She nodded. A man stepped away from the group clustered in the shadows far from the nearest street light. He went to seal off the only escape route.

The six others moved slowly toward the house, ceremonially sniffing the wind, pairing off without instruction, as if by instinct, into three teams.

Except for faint sounds deep in their throats, they made no more noise than a swamp maple leaf drifting down to land on a still pond.

Two went up the back fire escape and two up the escape on the side of the building. Sheila Feinberg, followed by another woman, ripped the lock from the front door and began up the stairway.

Inside the attic apartment, Chiun put a hand over Remo's mouth to still his breathing.

A moment later, he released it. "There are six," he said. "Be on your feet. We must be prepared to leave quickly."

Remo rose. As he got to his feet, pain hammered at his head. His throat and stomach, while healing from the rips Sheila Feinberg had made, felt as if only a thin sheet of tissue paper was holding in a throbbing, red-hot mass of hurt. He staggered slightly, then tried to breathe deeply, as Chiun pushed him gently into a corner of the room next to one of the windows leading to the side fire escape.

Chiun quickly lit three candles, set them in the center of the floor, then turned off the room lights.

"Why the candles, Chiun?" Remo asked.

"Shhhh," Chiun said.

They waited.

But not for long.

Mrs. Marjorie Billingham, chairman of the Good and Welfare Committee of St. Aloysius Roman Catholic Church, was a forty-year-old woman who had worried for the last ten years about, in order of importance, a straying husband, eye wrinkles, and ten extra pounds. She had now lost the eye wrinkles and was shedding the ten pounds on her new all-flesh diet. She no longer worried about her husband because if he ever cheated again, she would simply eat him. Mrs. Marjorie Billingham was the first one through.

She crashed through the glass of the side window, a murderous roar rumbling in her throat like the fast-growing sound of a forest fire. But the sound changed to a yelp as the knife mounted by Chiun across the glass pane drove itself through one no-longer-so-fatty breast and buried itself deep in her heart.

The animal scream of death was answered by growls from the front door and back window. Then

98

there was sneezing from outside the apartment door. Chiun reached behind him to touch Remo's hand.

A second figure loomed in the now broken side window. Chiun's blue-clad, kimonoed arm reached out and grabbed the person by the throat. Like popping a crumpled piece of paper into a wastebasket, he tossed her into the room. The woman turned a circle in the air and landed on all fours like a cat. She turned toward Chiun and Remo with a hiss, then her body remembered her throat had been torn out. She fell heavily to the floor and rolled once into the three lit candles.

Two of them overturned. Hot wax spilled onto an old newspaper on the floor which flared up as the candle flame touched it. Paper and wax crackled into bright flame as Chiun pushed Remo out the side window in front of him.

"Up," he ordered. Remo began up the metal steps to the roof of the building.

Chiun stood in the opening of the window, covering Remo's retreat, as the front door burst open and Sheila Feinberg jumped into the room. At the same moment, the back windows shattered and two forms jumped into the room. Their faces were distorted. Their teeth showed in evil rictus, made more gruesome by the flash and play of the light on their faces from the crackling spreading fire.

Another woman pushed into the room behind Sheila Feinberg. All stood rooted in their tracks. The fire from the paper had spread to a corner of the bed sheet and from there to a wad of cotton, soaked in a pine oil, which Chiun had used to clean Remo's wounds.

Dried-out wallpaper behind the bed began burning almost instantly. The room was illuminated like a light show, with dancing flames casting red, yellow and blue glows around the room. The four, human tigers growled again and moved a step forward, toward their own dead, toward Chiun, but a flash of flame stopped them. Chiun darted out the window and followed Remo up the fire escape. Behind him, the snapping of flames grew in volume and intensity.

As Chiun vaulted the convex tile, topping the wooden railing that ran around the top of the frame building, he looked down and saw a lick of flame tongue its way out the broken window. Faintly, Remo could hear the yowling of cats, as if in distress.

He puffed like a fat man carrying a load as Chiun came to him.

"They will not follow," Chiun said. "We will cross to the next building and then go down." He added, almost gently, "Are you able to, my son?"

"Lead on," said Remo with a jaunty sureness he did not feel. His legs ached from the brief climb up the fire escape. His arms hurt from the effort of pulling himself over the wooden railing surrounding the roof. His stomach felt as if it had been hammered on all day and the wounds were ready to begin bleeding again. He hoped the distance between the two buildings was not far. If it was more than a step, he could not make it.

It was only a step and Chiun went across first. He turned to give Remo a hand, froze in position, then withdrew the hand. He turned to look across the roof toward the far corner where the shadows were deepest and the blackness most total. In the faint glimmer of the night sky, Remo saw it too. He stepped back onto the roof of the first building. There were two small dots of light in the corner of the next roof. They were eyes. Cat's eyes.

Chiun raised his arms out to his sides. The blue kimono sleeves draped down in heavy folds toward his waist.

The twin dots of light moved. They rose, as the tiger man moved from a crouch and stood tall, silhouetted now against the night sky. With a sound that was

100

half triumphant laugh, half happy purr, he moved forward.

James Hallahan, assistant director for the Boston office of the Federal Bureau of Investigation, said to Chiun, "And now you'll be a meal."

He moved forward slowly, toward the center of the roof, making no sound despite his big, strong body.

Chiun did not move. His arms were still raised as if to shield Remo.

"What is not man is less than man," Chiun said softly. "Leave us, creature."

"I'll leave your bones," Hallahan said and opened his throat to laugh.

He charged. With animal cunning he knew that the old Oriental would move aside from his charge. Then he would simply ignore him, vault the small step between buildings, and capture the young, white man to use as shield and hostage.

But Chiun did not move when Hallahan reached him. The kimonoed arms moved like windmill blades. They seemed slow, but there was a howl as one of Hallahan's extended arms broke with a loud crack, hit by Chiun's thin and bony arm as if it were a fast-moving two-by-four. Hallahan fell back momentarily, roared again and dove at Chiun, his good arm extended before him, teeth bared and head turned sideways, as if hoping to get his mouth close to Chiun's throat, to rip it out.

Behind him, Remo could hear the sound of flames growing louder and louder. Then below, in the small space between buildings, he saw a lick of flame spurt out through a small window in the hallway outside their attic apartment.

Hallahan was almost upon Chiun, his right hand in front of him, fingers curled into claws, almost in a kung fu pose. For a moment, it seemed as if he had buried Chiun under his size and weight. Then there was a string of little, snapping noises. Remo knew the sound of fingers breaking. Chiun's body dipped and Hallahan's own momentum carried him over Chiun's back and the edge of the roof. As he sailed past Remo, Remo could see his mouth still wide open, still anxious to bite. He felt a strange emotion. He had learned to be a Master of Sinanju, a master of men, but he was still civilized man and now was faced with an enemy who shared the killing blood lust of a jungle beast. The new emotion was simply fear.

He had no time to think about it. Even before Hallahan's body hit the paved yard below, Chiun was helping Remo to the next roof.

Coming across the buildings, from two streets away, Remo heard the sound of fire sirens.

The sounds had died when, a few minutes later, they sat in a taxicab heading for the outskirts of the city. Remo slumped against the hard seat of the cab and tried to close his eyes. Chiun kept looking through the back window, darting his glance back and forth, as if expecting to see a pack of wild animals in full-throated chase of Cab Number 2763-B, fifty cents for the first half mile, fifteen cents each additional fifth. Unless you take the group rate.

Later, in a motel room, Chiun put Remo gently on the bed and said, "The danger has passed."

"They didn't seem like much, Chiun. You handled them kind of easy," Remo said.

Chiun shook his head sadly. "They are tigers," he said, "but not yet tigers. They are cubs but when they are grown, we may all have much to fear. But it will not matter because we will not be here."

Remo turned his head and felt the pain of the movement in his injured throat.

"Oh? Where will we be?"

"We will not be here," Chiun repeated as if that were explanation enough.

"You said that."

"It is time to move on. We have done all we can for

this Constitution of yours and now must be on about our business."

"Chiun, this is our business. If these people . . . these things are going to be as bad as you say when they grow up, now is the time to stop them. Otherwise, we may not be safe anywhere."

Chiun's bland expression convinced Remo there was no flaw in the logic, but Chiun said stubbornly, "We are leaving."

"Wait a minute," said Remo. "It has something to do with the legend, doesn't it?"

"You should rest now."

"Not until I hear the legend," said Remo.

"Why is it, when I want you to heed the ancient wisdom of Sinanju, to read the records and learn the history, you ignore me. But now, when it is nothing, you bother me with foolish questions about a legend?"

"Nothing?" Remo said. "The legend?"

"I suspect I will never rest until I indulge your one-thought mind."

"You said it, Little Father. The legend."

"As you wish. But you know legends are like old maps. They are not always to be trusted. The world changes."

"But Sinanju goes on forever," Remo said. "The legend."

Chiun sighed. "It is really one of our least important legends, concerning as it does people of no worth."

"Then it's about me," Remo said.

Chiun nodded. "Sometimes you learn very quickly. When you do, it always surprises me."

"Get on with it, Chiun."

"All right." He began to mumble speedily, in Korean.

"In English," said Remo.

"The legends lose their flavor in English."

"And I lose their meaning in Korean. In English, please."

"Only because you say please. As you know, you are Shiva, the Destroyer."

"I don't know if I believe that," Remo said.

"See. I told you this legend is foolish and not worth the telling."

"Try me anyway."

"Then be quiet and do not interrupt. Whose legend is this anyway? You are Shiva, the Destroyer, avatar of the god of destruction."

"Right," said Remo. "None other but Shiva, that's me."

Chiun fixed him with a glance that would have curled plate glass. Remo closed his eyes.

"You have not always been Shiva. The story is told of the Master of Sinanju, a wise, good, and gentle man. . . ."

"You, right?"

"A gentle and good man everybody takes advantage of finds among the white barbarians a man who was once dead. This creature is the dead night tiger made whole by the Master of Sinanju," Chiun said.

"When did I get to be a god? That's the part I like."

"Only after the wasting of much wisdom on you by the Master of Sinanju did you become Shiva. It is just a legend, after all."

Remo, who had "died" in a phony electric chair after being framed for a murder he did not commit, was resurrected to work for CURE as a man who did not exist. He nodded.

"The legend says you have been through death before and now can be sent to death again only by . . ." He stopped.

"Only by who, Chiun?" asked Remo.

"The legend is vague." Chiun shrugged. "Only by your kind or my kind."

Ignoring the pain in his stomach, Remo rolled on his side to look at Chiun.

"Now what the hell does that mean? Your kind and my kind? That's white men and yellow men. That means two-thirds of the world can kill me."

"Not exactly," Chiun said. "The legend is more detailed than that."

"Then be detailed. What's your kind and my kind?"

"My kind are from the village of Sinanju. Even the lowliest from my humble village, if given the opportunity, can slay you. Which is as it should be considering what you have allowed yourself to become."

"Can the editorial comment. And what's my kind? Ex-cops framed for murder? Government employees? Everybody from Newark, New Jersey? What's my kind?"

"Not those," Chiun said.

"Who then?"

"Not who, what. The legend says that even Shiva must walk with care when he passes the jungle where lurk other night tigers."

"And you think this Doctor Feinberg and her gang of vampires. . . ."

"They are cubs yet, Remo. I do not want you here when they grow up."

"Chiun, that's the worst pack of bullshit I ever heard."

"I am glad you feel that way, Remo. As soon as you are a little better, we will go somewhere to discuss it. Somewhere far away."

Remo suddenly felt tired, too tired to answer. He closed his eyes and fell asleep. The last thought on his mind was not concerning Sheila Feinberg and her pack, but a deep, abiding desire for a cigarette. Without filter. Packed with lung-rotting tars and nicotines.

CHAPTER EIGHT

He was not to sleep for long.

"Remo, how do you make this thing let you talk to Smith?" Remo opened an eye. Chiun was pointing a long, index finger at the telephone. His finger quivered, as if personally enraged at the thought of having to use the instrument. The finger contained all the outrage in the world, as if it were trying to shame an ant which had just climbed into the noodle salad.

"At this hour?" Remo said sleepily. "You going to start negotiating a new contract? Because tigers aren't covered under your old one?"

"We are not amused at your feeble attempts to be funny. How?"

"It's very easy," said Remo thickly, sleep still fuzzing his brain. "What day of the week is this?"

"Tuesday, Wednesday, the way you name them, who knows?" Chiun said.

"Well, you've got to know before you can call Smith. That's the key to the whole dippy system."

"All right. It is Wednesday."

"And does this month have an R in it?" asked Remo.

"May does not have an R in it. So how do I call Smith?"

"Well, as long as this is Wednesday and the month doesn't have an R in it, you just dial the 800 area code then the first seven digits of my old army serial number. If it had an R in it, you'd have to look in the *Wall Street Journal* for the total number of shares traded on the Big Board and dial the first seven numbers of that."

"What is this board that has shares?" asked Chiun.

"The Big Board. That's the New York Stock Exchange."

"Why did they pick that? They are truly lunatics."

"Ah," said Remo. "Now you're falling into the trap I always fall into. Instead of just doing it and making the call, I always wonder why they picked the New York Stock Exchange and not the Amex or Chicago Options Board. I get to wondering about things like that and before you know it, I forget the code or it's after midnight and the code has changed to something else and I don't remember it. Smith says that this is the product of a restless mind."

"Smith is wrong as usual," said Chiun. "It is the product of no mind at all. This is Wednesday in May without an R so how do I get to talk to Smith?"

"I told you. Dial 800 and then the first seven digits of my old army serial number."

"And that is?"

"Now you know why I never call Smitty on Wednesday. I don't remember my old army serial number. Call him tomorrow."

"Tomorrow may be too late," Chiun said softly.

But Remo wasn't listening. He had turned to the wall and sleep enveloped him like a fast-breaking wave. He slept with heavy, labored breaths. To

Chiun, for whom breathing was the secret key to the art and science of Sinanju, the noisy gasps told him how far Remo had slipped because of his injuries and how far he would have to come to return to condition.

If he had the time.

He lifted the telephone and dialed 0 for operator.

Dr. Harold W. Smith had spent the night in his office, reading the latest reports from Boston. There could no longer be any doubt. Dr. Sheila Feinberg had created more of the very same creatures she had become.

The rising toll of deaths proved that; separated by distance but not by time, they were the work of more than one.

Now, in a population where wits had already been scrambled by fright, there would be worse outcry with the mysterious death of James Hallahan, the assistant FBI director for Boston. A house had burned and in the charred ruins, firemen found the bodies of two persons. In the backyard, Hallahan's body was found. He may have been tracking the tiger people, been discovered and fell off the roof while trying to flee.

But why hadn't he been wearing shoes?

Still no word from Remo and Chiun. The days dragged. Smith was being forced to face the prospect that his two strongest weapons, Remo and Chiun, had gotten in the way of the tiger people and been . . .

Eaten?

Could it be? Remo and Chiun? A meal for someone?

Harold W. Smith allowed no antic thoughts to cross his mind and disrupt his usual pattern of precise logical thinking. But he could not block out the picture of Remo and Chiun, on a platter, lying on a table, surrounded by people drooling with anticipation.

Smith laughed. In that brief, fleeting, uncharacteristic act, Smith finally came to understand something he had never before allowed himself to consider.

He did not believe that Remo was the reincarnation of Shiva. That was a fairy tale of Chiun's. But he now knew he believed Remo and Chiun were indestructible. These two very real, very human people had stood for Smith and for CURE against diseases, nuclear weapons, the forces of the universe, gunmen, arsenals and electronic devices. They had always prevailed.

And would prevail again.

If they didn't, then no one could. The human race was doomed, and no amount of worrying would change that fact.

So Harold Smith discarded worry, for perhaps the first time in his adult life, and laughed again. Aloud.

His secretary, hearing the strange sound, thought Smith was choking and came running into the room.

"Are you all right, Doctor?"

"Yes, Miss Purvish," Smith said and snickered. "Ho ho, I'm fine and everything's going to be all right. Don't you ... ha ha ha ... think so?"

His secretary nodded and made a mental note. She would have to report Smith's unusual behavior to the person at the National Foundation for Scientific Research who paid her to telephone every month and report on Dr. Smith's mental health.

She had never met the person and never knew why anyone would think it was worth $100 a month to know the state of Smith's mind. But she liked the hundred dollars.

If she had been told the truth, that Smith himself paid her that money, she would not have believed it. But that was the way CURE operated, with thousands of people passing along tips to the FBI, the Agriculture Department, the Immigration Service, the Customs Bureau, pouring them all into a pipeline that

110

carried information. And at the end of the pipeline, watching all the reports, were CURE's computers. And Harold W. Smith. Checking everything.

But who checked the checker?

Early on, Smith had realized the almost absolute and unbridled power of his position could be enough to distort a man's logical judgment. If he suffered from an error in judgment, would he be able to tell? Impaired judgment might make it impossible to recognize impaired judgment.

So he devised the simple idea of having Miss Purvish pass along regular reports on his attitude and behavior. The reports bypassed the National Foundation for Scientific Research and went directly to Smith who had an opportunity generally unknown in a large organization—the chance to see what his secretary really thought of him.

For ten years she thought he was perfectly normal, normal being unemotional, penny-pinching and totally devoid of a sense of humor. Ten years, 520 reports, reading. "Subject perfectly normal."

He knew what the next report would read. "Subject laughed. Strange, unheard-of behavior."

The fact that laughter was unheard-of behavior for Harold Smith struck him as so funny he laughed again and kept laughing until Miss Purvish buzzed him on the intercom.

"Sorry to bother you with this, Doctor, but there is a phone call I can't make heads or tails of. I think it's for you."

"Yes?"

"As near as I can tell, we have fourteen telephone operators on the line at once, along with somebody speaking a language I can't understand. Everybody seems to be trying to reach some kind of emperor named Smith because if they don't they're going to be killed. I really don't understand it, sir."

111

Smith giggled. "Neither do I," he lied, "but I'll take it. I need a good laugh."

"Yes, sir. I guess so, sir," she said.

Another item for her report on Harold Smith's rapidly deteriorating mental condition.

"Hello," he said and was deluged with a gabbling gaggle of operators all talking at once. He could not understand a single word until he heard a regal roar.

"Silence, cackling hens. Remove yourselves from my hearing."

It was Chiun's voice. Like clicking a switch, the line cleared and he and Smith could talk uninterrupted. Smith pressed a button that made it impossible for Miss Purvish to listen in.

"Hello," Smith said.

"Greetings to the Emperor from the Master of Sinanju," said Chiun.

"Are you all right?" Smith asked. "Remo?"

"I am well as ever. Remo is not."

"What's wrong?"

"He has been injured by one of those people beasts. We must return to Folcroft."

"No," Smith said quickly. "That's too dangerous. We can't do that."

"Last night they attacked and tried to kill us. Soon they may succeed. We must be gone from this city of beans and people who do not know how to speak."

"Last night?" Smith said. "Was that the building where there was the fire?"

"Yes."

"There was a body found in the yard. An FBI man, Hallahan. Do you know what happened to him?"

"Yes. I removed him."

Smith felt a sinking feeling in his stomach. "Why?" he asked.

"He was one of them," Chiun said. "They are now many."

"Oh."

"We must return to Folcroft where Remo can be safe."

"Where are you now?" Smith asked.

"In a hotel you drive to," Chiun said.

"A motel. How'd you got there?"

"By a taxicab driven by a driver who mercifully did not speak once."

"They'll find you then," Smith said. "The cabdriver will remember both of you."

"Yes. We must return to Folcroft. If that is forbidden, we will leave the country, never to return."

"No. All right," Smith said.

He gave Chiun elaborate plans on taking a taxi to one of the entrances of the Massachusetts Turnpike and there transferring to a rented limousine. That rented limousine from Boston would be met on the road by another rented limousine from Connecticut which would finish the trip to Folcroft.

"Do you understand all that?"

"Yes," Chiun said. "One thing more, Emperor, but so small as almost not to trouble you over."

"What is that?"

"Who is going to pay for all these cabs and limousines?"

"I will," Smith said.

"Do I have to advance the drivers the money?" asked Chiun.

"It would be helpful."

"I will get it back from you?" asked Chiun.

"Yes."

"I will get receipts," Chiun said and hung up.

Smith replaced the telephone. He no longer felt like laughing.

CHAPTER NINE

Sheila Feinberg paced back and forth next to the cool brick wall of the big stone-floored, empty warehouse. She slipped off her low-heeled leather shoes. It felt better to have the pads of her feet touching the floor.

"Where did they go?" she demanded.

"I traced them to the Colony Days Inn," a man said. When he spoke the other eight people inside the garage looked at him. They all squatted on the floor in a semicircle as Sheila paced in front of them.

"And?" she said.

"They are gone from there," the man said. He yawned, a large yawn, not a signal of fatigue, instead, the gulping demand for more oxygen typical of large animals which do not get enough exercise.

"Where did they go?" Sheila asked. She turned toward the wall as if counting the bricks, scratched down them with her fingernails in a brief show of anger, then wheeled around.

"We have to get them," she said. "That's all. We

have to get them. I want that young one. If only Hallahan hadn't fallen off that roof. He could find out."

"I found out," said the man with a brief display of pique. Sheila spun her head toward him as if he were attacking her. He met her eyes for a moment, then settled deeper onto his haunches and lowered his head. He spoke without looking up.

"They took a cab to the Massachusetts Turnpike and transferred to a limousine. I talked to the driver of the cab. The limousine was from Boston and was headed South. I have to wait for the limousine driver to get back to find out where he took them."

"Stay with it," Sheila ordered curtly. She added, "I know you'll do a good job."

The man looked up, smiling contentedly as if someone had stroked his neck. It was good to be noticed and praised. Especially by the leader of your pack.

It might even mean, that night, that he would get first feeding rights. Before all the good parts were gone.

CHAPTER TEN

The sun poured in through the one-way window of the hospital room. Beyond the window were the dark gray waters of Long Island Sound, now as flat as slate on a typical breezeless, airless New York City day. The humidity made people on the street feel as if a towel had been pulled from boiling water and dropped onto their faces.

Inside the room was the coolness of an air conditioner. As Remo woke up, he noticed it and noticed also that, for the first time in many years, he did not smell the faint charcoal flavor that air conditioning pumped into one's lungs.

He blinked his eyes and looked around.

Smith was sitting in a chair alongside his bed. He looked relieved to see Remo awake. His usual pinched-lemon look was replaced by the look of a lemon that had not yet been cut or squeezed. For Smith, whole lemon was happy; pinched, twisted, cut, squeezed, and juiced lemon was normal.

"You don't know how much fun it is to wake up and see you sitting there," said Remo, surprised by the thickness of his own voice. He usually didn't sleep that heavily. "I mean, some people wake up and see the woman they love. Or the surgeon who just saved their lives after a four-day operation. I see you, sitting there like a boa constrictor waiting to corner a mouse. It fills the heart with cheer."

"I've seen your wounds," said Smith. "You're lucky to see anyone."

"Oh, those," said Remo. "Chiun took care of them." He looked again around the room. "Where is he anyway?"

"He went down to the gymnasium. He said something about wanting to see the place where everything started to go wrong for him. I think it was the gymnasium where you two first met," Smith said dryly.

"Yeah. Well, forget that. Listen, have you got a cigarette?"

"Sorry, I don't smoke. I gave it up when the surgeon general's report came out. I thought you represented all the danger to my health I could handle."

"It's nice to be home," Remo said. "Holler out in the hall and get me a cigarette, will you?"

"Since when have you been smoking?"

"On and off. Every so often," Remo lied. He really wanted that cigarette and could not understand why. It had been years since he had smoked. Years of training had finally brought him to understand breathing was everything. All the tricks, all the magic, all the skill of Sinanju were built on breathing. Without it, nothing was possible. With it, nothing was impossible. The first thing one learned was not to breathe smoke.

But he wanted the cigarette nevertheless.

Smith nodded and went into the hall. While he was gone, Remo inspected the room. He realized, with a little shock, it was the same one in which he had awakened after being saved from the gimmicked electric chair.

Sentiment? For old time's sake? Not from Smitty. Remo was in that room because that room had been vacant. If the only vacancy had been in the boiler room, Remo would have been sleeping in the furnace between shovelfuls of coal.

It was the usual hospital room. White. One bed, one chair, one bureau, one window. But the window was a sheet of one-way glass through which Remo could see, but which was a mirror from the outside.

Smith came back with two cigarettes. "You owe them to the nurse in the hall. I told her you'd give them back to her. She said it was all right, but I told her you'd return them tomorrow. By the way, she thinks your name is Mr. Wilson and that Chiun is your valet."

"Don't tell him that," Remo said and yanked the cigarettes from Smith's hand. One slipped and fell to the floor.

Remo put the filtered cigarette to his mouth. Smith lit it from a book of matches that had exactly two matches. Remo wondered sometimes if the man was human. Two cigarettes, two matches. Smith could have taken an hour, walking the corridors looking for somebody with a free pack of matches with only two matches left in it.

Remo took his first huge inhale as Smith retrieved the other cigarette from the floor and put it, along with the remaining match, in the bureau next to Remo's bed.

The first taste made Remo cough. Had it always tasted so bad? He knew it had. Back when he had been smoking, he often quit, sometimes for weeks at a

119

time. That first puff when he weakened and went back was always a choking cough-producer, like the body's last shout of warning before surrender. The second puff was better and halfway through the cigarette it was as if he had never stopped, not even for an hour. It was that way again.

"Try to get me a pack, will you?" Remo said. "Put it on my room bill."

"I'll see what I can do," Smith said, then briefed Remo on what was happening in Boston.

The killings were continuing. Police had shot one of the tiger people. "It was a housewife. Unfortunately, she died so we didn't get a chance to study her and see if there's an antidote."

"That's a shame," Remo said.

"Now they're screaming for massive Federal intervention, and with you and Chiun out of it, I guess there's no alternative. What happened to you anyway?" asked Smith.

"I was in a car with one of them. I think it was Sheila Baby, even though she looked different. She slashed my throat and tried to rip out my stomach. She did a pretty good job."

"What about her?"

"I bopped her up some, but she got away," Remo said.

Smith felt a weight plummet from his gullet into his stomach. Remo was his best and had almost been killed. What hope did anyone else have? There was no limit to the number of tiger people Sheila Feinberg could make. Now each one of her pack was a new source of genetic material for others. The only way out would be to kill all the pack and make sure to eliminate Sheila Feinberg. Without her scientific knowledge, the geometric progression would stop.

But who could do it? If not Remo, who? Martial law, if imposed, was hardly likely to turn up Sheila and her tiger people. They looked like ordinary humans. FBI agent Hallahan proved that. On the day he had tried to kill Remo and Chiun, he had been working at his desk, just as he had every other day.

But if they weren't stopped and soon, before long, it would not be just Boston in peril. They could get in a car or on a plane and go anywhere in the country, anywhere in the world. You couldn't put the whole planet earth under martial law.

And even if you could, it probably wouldn't work.

The key was getting Sheila Feinberg first. That would stop the creation of new monsters. Then the existing ones could be hunted to ground, slowly but surely.

"Are you going to go back after her?" Smith asked. "Will you be able to?"

"Huh?" said Remo. He had not been listening. He was watching smoke rise from the glowing tip of the cigarette, savoring the taste.

"Can you go back after Feinberg, I said?"

"I don't know," Remo said. "I'm pretty weak. I seem to have lost my edge. And I don't think Chiun would let me go. He's pretty spooked about some kind of legend."

"Chiun is always disturbed about some legend or other," Smith said.

"Even if I found her again, I don't know what I could do with her," Remo said. "I couldn't get her the last time."

"You could call for help," Smith said.

Remo looked at him, angrily for a moment, as if Smith had attacked his competence. Then the look faded. After all, why not call for help? If he ever met Sheila again, he would need it.

"I don't know, Smitty," he said.

"Why did they come after you anyway?" Smith asked. "I mean, they shouldn't have thought you posed some kind of special threat to them. Even after you wounded Feinberg. Why not just leave you

121

alone? If they're really animals, revenge doesn't make any sense. That's human, not animal. Animals escape danger. They don't go back just to get even."

"Maybe they just like me. Me and my winning ways," Remo said.

"Dubious, dubious. Highly dubious," Smith said as Remo sucked one last lungful of smoke, saw the cigarette's glow reach the plastic filter which melted from white threads into dried tan glue, and stubbed the butt out in the ashtray.

"I'll leave you now," said Smith.

"Don't forget that pack of cigarettes," Remo said, but Smith did not hear him.

He was staring at a problem to which he already knew the answer but did not want to face.

He was hunting the Sheila Feinberg pack and the pack was hunting Remo. To get them, he would have to use Remo as bait.

It was clear and logical and left no alternatives. It was risk Remo, or risk the rest of the country, the rest of the world.

Smith knew what he had to do. It was what he had always done. His duty.

The trap was set with a classified advertisement in the Boston *Times*.

"S.F. Patient is at Folcroft, Rye."

There was little subtlety about the trap and when one of her pack showed the ad to Sheila Feinberg, she knew it for what it was.

"It's a trap," she said.

"So we'll ignore it," said the other woman, a buxom brunette with narrow hips and long legs. "There is plenty of meat in Boston."

But the age-old instinct of survival before all else gave way in Sheila Feinberg to another instinct—the longing to reproduce one's kind. She smiled sweetly

122

at the woman, showing long white teeth that looked as if they had been polished by chewing through soft bone and said, "No. We won't ignore it. We will go. I want that man."

CHAPTER ELEVEN

Remo looked at the high ceiling of the Folcroft gymnasium, its climbing ropes lashed up like a telephone circuit's cluster of wires, then scuffed the tip of his Italian loafer across the highly varnished floor.

"This is where we first met," Chiun said. He wore a yellow morning robe and looked about the gymnasium as if it were a favored son.

"Yeah," said Remo. "And I tried to kill you."

"That is correct," said Chiun. "Right then I knew there was something about you I might be able to tolerate."

"But I wasn't able to do it and you slapped me down good," Remo said.

"I remember. It was very satisfying."

"You would think so," said Remo.

"And then I taught you karate tricks and made them seem important."

"I never understood why you did that, Chiun,"

Remo said. "What did karate have to do with Sinanju?"

"Nothing. But I knew these lunatics would never give me enough time to teach you anything correctly. So I gave you karate, which I thought you might be able to remember. But if I had said, this is karate it is useless foolishness for attacking anything except a piece of soft pine shelving would you have listened? No. One must always feel that a gift has some value. I told you that karate was wonderful, marvelous, and would make you invincible. Then I proved it by attacking boards and doing tricks. Only that way could I manage to capture your attention for the five minutes a day necessary to teach you that game. How did they ever manage to toilet train you, Remo, when you forget everything so quickly?"

"Can that, Little Father. And then I left you and went out to kill the recruiter."

Chiun nodded. "Yes. He was a good man, Mac-Cleary. He had courage and intelligence."

"He picked me," Remo said.

"He had almost enough courage and intelligence to overcome his lapses in judgment," Chiun said.

"Since then it's been you and me, Chiun. How many years?"

"Twenty-seven," Chiun said.

"It hasn't been twenty-seven. Ten. Twelve. Fourteen outside," Remo said.

"It seems like twenty-seven," Chiun said. "I started out a young man. I gave you my youth, my best years. They have been frittered away in irritation, annoyance, a lack of true and proper respect, wasted on someone who eats meat and sneaks cigarettes like a child."

Remo, who did not know that Chiun had noticed his smoking, said quickly, "It was only a couple. I wanted to see how they tasted after all these years."

"How did they taste?"

"Wonderful," Remo said.

"You give up the breathing so you can inhale particles of burning horse dung? This is truth, Remo, they make those things from horse and cow droppings."

"They make them from tobacco and, no, I don't mean to give up my breathing. Can't I do both?"

"How can you breathe? Breathing involves air but your big white mouth is busy taking in smoke. They only tell you they make them out of tobacco. It is horse and cow droppings. This is the American way, the big profit that makes your whole country work."

"You sound like a Communist."

"Do they smoke cigarettes?" asked Chiun.

"Yes. Made from horse and cow droppings. I've had them."

"Then I am no Communist. Just a poor, underpaid, misunderstood teacher who has failed to win the respect of his student."

"I respect you, Chiun."

"Quit smoking."

"I will."

"Good."

"Tomorrow."

In front of Chiun a pair of gymnastic rings hung from ceiling ropes. Without turning toward Remo, he swiped his hands at the hard plastic rings. They swung past him, their speed a blur, aimed at Remo's head like a boxer's one-two punch. Remo saw the one coming from the right side first. He slipped to the left to avoid it, and was hit in the forehead by the ring moving from the left. As he straightened up, the right ring, returning to its starting position hit him in the back of the head.

Chiun looked at him with disgust.

"Keep smoking. When they come for you, they will have you like a pork chop."

"You that sure they'll come for me?" asked Remo, rubbing his head.

"They will come. You are without hope. And don't ask me to help because I can't stand your breath."

He walked past Remo, out of the gymnasium. Remo, still rubbing his head, looked at the gently swinging rings and wondered if he had lost that much of his edge already.

Smith posted extra guards in the corridor outside Remo's room and distributed photos of Dr. Sheila Feinberg to be posted on the wall of Folcroft's gatehouse. If the woman appeared, she was to be admitted without question but Smith was to be notified at once.

Smith thought of assigning a personal bodyguard to Remo to stay with him all the time, but realized Chiun would regard it as an insult. Assigning a guard to Remo, with Chiun around, would be like adding a Boy Scout patrol to the Seventh Army for added firepower.

There was nothing to do but wait. Smith did, in his office, reading the latest reports on two more deaths in Boston during the night. The governer had just declared martial law, which meant the city would be almost as well protected and patrolled as it had been before policemen were required to practice psychiatry, social work, and redemption. If Dostoyevsky were alive today, he thought, he would have entitled his masterpiece just *Crime*. *Crime and Punishment* would have no meaning to most of the general public. They had never heard of punishment.

Smith waited.

There had been nine years of hard decisions, made cleanly and promptly. Now, when it had all been done and had come to this, Jacki Bell couldn't decide whether to wear the man-tailored brown suit, which had the virtue of being professional-looking, or the yellow scoop-neck dress, which had the virtue of being cool.

She opted for cool and as she dressed thought how lucky she had been. Lucky enough to get out of a debilitating marriage, lucky enough to stay afloat financially during school years, lucky and smart enough to tough it out and become Jacki Bell, B.A., Jacki Bell, M.A., and finally Jacqueline Bell, Ph.D.

Dr. Jacqueline Bell.

Her luck still held, right up to reading the American Psychoanalytical Journal and finding the advertisement for a job at Folcroft Sanatarium. There had been many applicants but she'd been lucky enough to get the job from Doctor Smith.

If anybody asked her who she thought should be her first patient in therapy at Folcroft, she would pick Harold W. Smith without hesitation.

Throughout the interview he had spoken without looking at her. He had been reading some kind of reports that came in over a computer terminal on his desk. He had stared at a telephone as if expecting it to leap in the air and try to strangle him. He had drummed pencils, looked out his strangely brown-tinted windows, and finally, after asking her the same question three times, told her the job was hers.

As she inspected herself in the full-length mirror on the back of the bedroom door in the three-room apartment she'd been lucky to find, she shrugged. There were worse cases in the world than Doctor Smith, she supposed. At least he had enough sanity left to hire her.

She had tried to find out what his doctorate was in because he did not have M.D. after his name on the door. But he had not volunteered any information, except to tell her she would be on her own. He would not look over her shoulder. He would not question her professional decisions, and in fact would be most happy if he never had to talk to her again.

That would be okay with her too. He'd get no complaints from her. She counted herself lucky to get the job.

It used to be that a bachelor's degree would guarantee a job. Then college classrooms turned into places that ladled out "relevant education"—like courses in soap opera for students who could barely read and write—and the B.A. was devalued. It took a master's degree to get a job. Then the same thing happened to the master's degree.

So it took a Ph.D. to get a job. But only for awhile. Soon it too was considered worthless. People who hired others went back to using Tennessee Windage and simple reading and writing tests to determine what potential employee might be able to find his way to work in the morning without a keeper. No degree guaranteed a job any more because no degree guaranteed that its holder had an education that went beyond one-two-three-many.

The only good thing about it all, Jacki Bell reflected, was that the doctors of education who started it all were in the same bag. They found their doctorates were meaningless too and they had trouble getting work. Of course, being educated men, they decided they had nothing to do with it. It was all the fault of the evil, corrupt, capitalist society.

She remembered something she had read once in a book of political essays: "He who creates the deluge often gets wet."

Dr. Jacqueline Bell approved of her image in the mirror and brushed imaginary lint off her left shoulder.

The doorbell rang.

She was not expecting anyone but it might be someone from the sanitarium. Because she had not grown up in New York City, Chicago, or Los Angeles, she went right to the door and opened it without asking who was there.

A woman stood there, a beautiful woman with long

130

blonde hair, eyes that slanted in an almost feline fashion, and a body so breathtakingly and breakneckedly poured into her clothes she made Jacki feel instant-tacky. The woman smiled showing the most perfect white teeth Jacki had ever seen.

"Doctor Bell?" the woman asked.

Jacki nodded.

"I'm glad to meet you. I'm Doctor Feinberg."

"Oh. Are you from Folcroft?"

"Yes. They asked me to stop by and pick you up on my way in this morning."

"This is my lucky day," Jacki said. "It's so hot out there I don't relish the walk." She stood aside and waved Dr. Feinberg into the apartment. "We're early by the way," Jacki said. "Have you eaten yet? Why not have a bite with me?"

Sheila Feinberg's smile broadened as she entered the apartment.

"Exactly what I had in mind," she said.

Chiun said "Why are those people in blue uniforms in the halls? Did you put them there?"

"That is correct, Master of Sinanju," Smith said formally.

"Why?" asked Chiun. He had stopped calling Smith "emperor." It seemed appropriate when he was away from Folcroft and met Smith infrequently. But close up, Chiun dropped the convention lest Smith think it was an acknowledgement that Smith was of higher rank than Chiun.

"Because I am worried that those people might find Remo. I want him protected."

"How could they find him here?" asked Chiun.

"Because I have told them he is here," Smith said.

"That is a very good reason," Chiun said slowly.

"Chiun, we have to get these creatures. I know you may be upset because I'm possibly endangering

131

Remo's life. But I have to look at more than that. I have to think of the whole country."

"And on its own, how many Masters of Sinanju has this wonderful country produced?" Chiun asked.

"On its own, none," Smith said.

"And you think the country is worth Remo's life nevertheless?"

"If you put it on those terms, yes," Smith said.

"Worth Remo's and mine?" asked Chiun.

"Yes."

"Remo's, mine, and yours?" Chiun persisted.

Smith nodded.

"How many lives does it take before it is no longer worth those lives?" Chiun spat on the floor of Smith's office. "Remo's life just because some fat people in some chilly city got themselves eaten?"

"It's not just them and not just Boston. Unless we can stop these . . . these creatures, it could spread nationwide. Worldwide. Perhaps even to Sinanju."

"Sinanju will be safe," Chiun said.

"They can even get to Korea, Chiun."

"But Sinanju exists where Remo and I exist. Where we are, there is Sinanju. I will see that Remo stays safe," Chiun said. "For you and your emperor there may be no safety, but Remo and I will survive."

For a moment, the two men's eyes locked, until Smith turned away from Chiun's burning hazel eyes.

"I wanted to ask you something," he said. "Remo just doesn't seem right. It's not just that he's injured," Smith said. "He's smoking. And last night he ate a steak. When was the last time he ate any meat besides duck and fish? What is happening to him. Chiun?"

"His body has suffered a shock from his injuries, a shock so great his body has forgotten what it is."

Smith looked puzzled. "I don't understand."

"Sometimes, when someone suffers mental shock, they have what you call the forget disease."

132

"Amnesia," Smith suggested.

"Yes. The body may suffer the same illness. Remo's has. His body is returning to where it was before I undertook his training. There is no way of stopping it from happening."

"Does that mean . . . does that mean that's it for him? That Remo's done? His special skills are done?"

"No one knows that," said Chiun. "His body may return all the way to where he began or may stop only part of the way there. It may stop anywhere and never again change or may reach bottom then return to what it was before his injury. There is no way to tell because each man is different."

"Yes, I know."

"I would think you forgot," Chiun said, "since you regard Remo as just another man, just another target for these tiger people, without considering he is a Master of Sinanju too."

Chiun's eyes narrowed with intensity. Smith could feel, as he so often did when dealing with Remo and Chiun, that he faced an elemental life-and-death force. Smith suspected he was on a swaying bridge.

"Fortunately, he's Shiva, the Destroyer God, isn't he?"

He essayed a small smile, pushing it into the conversation like inadequate seed money.

"Yes, he is," said Chiun. "But even the dead night tiger can be victim to the tiger people. What happens to him will be on your hands, and your head. Now, if you would be wise, you will keep those guards and their guns away from Remo's room because I will be there."

Chiun had stood during the conversation. Now he spun and walked away, red robe trailing behind as if he were a bride racing down the aisle of a church because she was late and they'd started the wedding without her.

He turned back at the door. "When Remo is well

enough, he and I are leaving. You will deal with your tiger people yourself because he will be elsewhere."

"Where will you go?" Smith asked glumly.

"Anywhere. Out of your employ."

Sheila Feinberg restrained herself from laughing aloud when she saw the picture of herself in the guard's building just inside the large, stone wall surrounding Folcroft Sanitarium.

It was a picture of the old Sheila Feinberg with hook nose, saggy eyes, and the desperate hairdo. It told Sheila clearly, and not without some shock, how ugly she had been before the changeover. It told her too that Folcroft was one giant trap waiting to spring shut.

"Who's that, your wife?" Sheila asked the guard, a gaunt man with a disproportionate beer belly and sweat rings showing on his blue shirt under his armpits.

"No, praise God," he said, smiling at the beautiful buxom blonde standing in front of him. "Just some dip we're supposed to keep an eye out for. Maybe an escaped patient or something. Look at her. She won't be back. Probably went and joined the circus." He smiled harder at Sheila. "Anyway, I'm not married," he lied.

Sheila nodded.

"Those kind of people will be your responsibility now, Doctor, I guess," the guard said. He looked again at the letter of appointment to the psychoservices division.

"This is all in order. What you do, Doctor, is go inside. Your division is in the right wing of the main building. When you get yourself organized, go get yourself an ID card. Then you won't have any more trouble at the gate. Of course, when I'm on, you won't have any trouble 'cause I'm not likely to forget you."

He handed back the letter. Sheila moved in closer to take it from him and brushed her body against his.

The guard watched her walk away and felt a tingle in his groin he hadn't felt since his second year of marriage, eight emotional centuries ago, a tingle he thought was no longer possible. Who knew? One thing he had learned from working at Folcroft was that shrinks were nuttier than the people they were supposed to treat. Maybe this one liked old skinny guards with big beer bellies. He looked at her name again on the sign-in sheet. Jacki Bell. Dr. Jacki Bell. It had a nice ring to it.

A white coat and clipboard are passports in any healing institution in the world. When she got them from a hall closet, Sheila Feinberg was free to roam Folcroft as she wished.

She quickly realized the big L-shaped main building was divided into two parts. The front section of the old brick structure was given over to the sanitarium's main business, treating patients. But the south wing, the base of the L, was different.

It housed computers and offices on the first floor. Upstairs where hospital rooms. On a lower level, built into the natural slope of the land, was a gymnasium that stretched almost to the back of Folcroft's property, where old boat docks gnarled like arthritic fingers into the still waters of Long Island Sound.

And sealing off the entire wing were guards.

At a different time in her life, Sheila Feinberg might have wondered just what was going on that required such security in a sanitarium, but she no longer cared about that. She cared about finding Remo, and she knew he was in the building's south wing.

Sheila went back to the main building and posed in the Special Services office for a Polaroid picture.

"Interesting place," she said to the young woman clerk who ran the office.

"Not bad. They leave you alone, which is better than some jobs I've had."

"My first day," Sheila said. "By the way, what's in the south wing that they have so many guards? Something special?"

"It's always like that. I hear from the grapevine they've got a special rich patient there." The girl cut the photograph's edges with a paper cutter and mounted the picture on a heavy card, using rubber cement. "They do some kind of government research over there, computers and stuff. I guess they don't want to take a chance on damaging the equipment."

Sheila was more interested in the special rich patient. "That rich man over there? Is he married?" she asked with a smile.

The young girl shrugged as she placed the photo card into a machine that looked like a credit card printer. She pressed a switch and the top of the machine lowered. There was a faint hiss of air and Sheila could smell the acrid fumes of heated plastic.

"I don't know if he's married. He's got his own servant with him. An old Oriental. Here you are, Doctor. Pin this on your coat and you can go anywhere."

"Even the south wing?"

"Anywhere. You can't treat your nut cases if you can't get to them," the girl said.

"Yeah," Sheila said. "Let me get at them."

Sheila skipped lunch in the main dining room and strolled down the rocky ground behind the buildings, leading to the old docks. They were obviously unused but still looked sturdy enough. She filed that information away in her head.

Looking back at the main building, she was surprised to see the glass in the south wing was mirrored one-way glass. People inside could see out, but no one outside could see in. She thought for a moment that the white man might even be watching her. The thought, instead of frightening her, made her tingle

136

with anticipation. She yawned, a big cat's yawn, then smiled at the second floor windows over the gymnasium building.

After lunch, her badge got her past the guards outside the second-floor entrance to the south wing. She was in an ordinary hospital corridor, exuding its traditional scent, Clorox and dead air.

She did not have to see Remo to know where he was. She smelled him as she walked along the narrow corridor. She followed the scent to a room near the end of the hall. The scent was Remo's but was somehow different. There was an acrid smell of something having been burned. She recognized it as cigarette fumes.

She neared Remo's door. For a moment the urge to push the door open and walk in was almost overpowering. She caught herself when she sensed another scent. It was the smell of jasmine and herbs. It came from the old Oriental. She had smelled it in the Boston attic apartment after she had cleared her nose of the pepper that had been sprinkled in the hallway.

The room number was 221-B. She went down another corridor and found a stairway that opened onto a fire escape leading down the outside of the building. At the corner of the building, the fire escape platform split and ran all around the outside of the patients' rooms on the second floor.

Perfect, she thought. Perfect, and she went back to the psychoservices department in the main building to kill some time and draw a plan.

In room 221-B, Chiun said to Remo, who was puffing gently on a cigarette, "They are here."

"Now how do you know that?" Remo asked. He was a little weary of Chiun's alarms about tiger people. What would be nice, he thought, would be a Caribbean vacation. And a large piña colada.

"The same way you would have known it but a week ago," Chiun said. "With my senses."

137

"Forget it," Remo said.

"They are here nonetheless," Chiun repeated dully. How could he save Remo from the tigers when Remo was not only unable to protect himself, but didn't even seem to care? Moments ago, footsteps in the hallway moved toward the door, stopped, then retreated rapidly. They were not the footsteps of a normal human. Instead of the infinitesimal time lag between putting down the heel and putting down the sole of the foot, these footsteps had come down with one faint, but continuous sound, as if the bottom of the foot were round and padded. Like a tiger's.

"You take care of them," Remo was saying. "I'm thinking about pork chops. And applesauce and mashed potatoes. Yeah, pork chops."

Three members of Sheila Feinberg's pack who had accompanied her to Rye, New York, entered Folcroft that night by going over the wall she told them at precisely the time she told them. Eight P.M., sharp.

At 8:12 P.M., they hit the corridor leading to Remo's room. The guard who had been stationed inside that hallway had been pulled off duty by Smith, at Chiun's demand. No one was there to stop the three as they sniffed and growled their way down the corridor toward Room 221-B where Remo lay in bed, his belly full of lobster and pork chop.

But the three were not unseen or unheard.

In Remo's room, Chiun rose from his small grass mat and moved so quietly toward the door, Remo did not hear him stir.

Dr. Smith in his office directly below the corridor, glanced at a television monitor and saw two women and a man walking down the hall. What he saw gave him a chill, the kind he had not felt since witnessing the results of Nazi atrocities in World War II.

The three tiger persons hunched over, their fingers almost touching the floor as they moved from closed door to closed door, sniffing. One turned, directly in front of the stationary, hall television camera. Her lips were pulled back exposing her teeth. Her eyes glinted inhumanly. Smith realized for the first time just how much animal and how little human these tiger people had become.

He yanked open his center desk drawer, grabbed a .45 caliber automatic and ran from his office to the flight of stairs leading to the upstairs corridor.

Chiun waited inside the door of the hospital room while Remo started to sit up in bed.

"They are here," Chiun said.

"I gathered that," Remo said.

"So what are you doing?" asked Chiun.

"Going to help."

"Help who do what? Rest your bloated belly."

"Just because I ate something good doesn't mean I can't help you," Remo said.

Chiun turned away in disgust, dismissing Remo with a wave of his hand.

Outside the door, the three tiger people scratched on the fire-retardant metal covering the wooden door. All they had to do was turn the knob to enter the room, but they did not. They scratched at it. Their fingernails made a soft insistent noise, like the mewing of cats left outside by mistake with night coming on.

They purred.

Smith pushed through the set of double fire doors leading to the corridor. He choked back a gasp at the sight of three persons scratching on the door. He moved to the corner of the hallway where he could not be surprised by anyone who might follow him through the doorway. He raised his gun and called out, "All right, all of you. Away from that door. Down on the floor."

The three turned to him. The expressions on their

faces would have been appropriate only if Harold W. Smith was a lamb chop.

Inside the hospital room, Chiun and Remo heard Smith's voice.

"What is that idiot doing here?" Chiun said.

The three members of Sheila Feinberg's pack moved away from the door toward Smith, their arms raised over their heads, fingers curled in imitation of deadly claws, mouths open and drooling.

"That'll do," Smith said coldly. "Hold it right there." The gun was unwavering in his right hand, near his hip.

The two women and a man kept moving toward him. Smith waited until they were away from the door and repeated his command.

"The three of you. Down on the floor."

But instead of dropping, the three separated and came at Smith, breaking into a run, charging, growling. Smith fired a shot which hit the man's chest and lifted him off his feet before plunking him back onto the marble floor.

In Room 221-B, Remo started up again from bed.

"That's Smitty. He needs help," he said.

"Get back in bed."

"Screw it, Little Father. I'm helping."

"You?" said Chiun disdainfully. "I will go." He pushed his way out into the hall, and left Remo sitting, strangely tired and empty, on the edge of the bed.

On the fire escape outside Remo's room, Sheila Feinberg rose to her feet from the position in which she had lain for the last four hours. She stretched once. Her muscles were loose and ready.

She looked through a tiny scratch she had found in the corner of the mirrored window in Remo's room and saw Chiun going out into the hallway.

As the door closed behind him, Sheila, with a running start, threw her body against the window, crashed through it, and landed gently on her feet alongside Remo's bed.

Remo looked at her with shock.

She purred at him.

"Hello, sweet meat," she said. "I've missed you."

In the hall, the two women crouched in front of Smith, separated from each other and from him by five feet. Smith seemed reluctant to fire. He covered first one, then the other with his automatic, and again ordered them to lie flat on the floor. They hissed.

Chiun saw tensing of the calf muscles protruding from under the women's skirts. The attack leap was impending.

Like a cold blue wind, he moved between the women and Smith.

He slapped the gun away from Smith's hand. It hit the floor with a loud metallic clank, like a hammer dropped onto ceramic tile. The women leaped at Smith but Chiun was between them and their target.

A raised left hand stopped one of the women as completely as if she had impaled herself full speed on a spear. The second woman turned her head to give her open mouth a clean bite at Chiun's throat. He merely slid below the woman's head and came up, almost casually, with an elbow into a point slightly above the pit of the woman's stomach. The air went out of her with a sibilant hiss and she fell onto the other woman.

Smith brushed past Chiun and knelt over the two women.

"They're dead," he said.

"Of course," said Chiun.

"I wanted them alive," Smith said.

"They wanted you dead," said Chiun. "Maybe they were wiser than you." He looked at them. "Neither is the one who was here earlier."

Chiun ran toward the hospital room, Smith following at his heels.

When they entered the room, it was empty.

Broken glass from the window cluttered the floor. Chiun ran to the window and looked out. On the ground below, running toward the docks behind Folcroft, was a woman. She carried Remo's body over her shoulder, seemingly without effort, like a big man carrying a small rug.

"Aiiiieee," Chiun screamed and leaped through the jagged glass of the window.

Smith leaned out the window in time to see Chiun leap over the fire escape railing, drop two stories to the ground and land, running. Smith clambered onto the fire escape, careful not to slash himself on the glass shards, and followed down the stairs.

Ahead he saw, docked at the pier, a twenty-nine-foot Silverton cabin cruiser, with outriggers and a Bimini top.

The woman dumped Remo into the back of the boat and slipped the bow line from a rusted old cleat at the end of the dock. Then she jumped aboard.

Chiun was now forty feet from the dock.

He was on the dock when the twin engines of the big boat roared and the craft skidded forward, its nose in the air, into the darkness dropping over the chill waters of the Sound.

A few moments later, Smith stood alongside Chiun, watching the boat, running without lights, vanish into the deepening night.

Smith felt required to put a hand on Chiun's shoulder.

The old man seemed not to feel it and, looking at him, Smith realized how small and frail was this eighty-year-old Korean who knew so much about so many things.

Smith squeezed Chiun's shoulder in friendship and

in the sharing sense of comradeship that comes to people who have suffered a mutual loss.

"My son is dead," Chiun said.

"No, Chiun. He's not dead."

"He will be dead," Chiun repeated. His voice was flat and soft as if shock had robbed his vocal cords of the ability to register even the slightest emotion. "Because he can no longer protect himself."

"He won't be dead," Smith said firmly. "Not if I have anything to say about it."

He turned and strode purposefully back to Folcroft headquarters. He had work to do and the night was young.

CHAPTER TWELVE

Remo, who had been knocked unconscious by a right hand blow to the head by Sheila Feinberg, a right hand he never saw, came to as the power boat reversed its engines to bring itself to a stop. He felt the boat bump against another boat.

As he shook his head, trying to clear his vision, he felt Sheila's strong hand grip his right biceps, squeezing hard. It hurt.

"Come on," she said and pushed him to the rail of the Silverton cabin cruiser.

It was dark now and the salt smell from the Sound was stronger, as if the daylight's passing had removed a lid from it. Sheila helped Remo across the railing of her boat to another, smaller speed boat. All the while, she held his arm.

Remo decided enough was enough. He yanked his arm away. But it didn't work. Her fingers, like talons, still bit into his muscle.

Was he really that weak, he wondered. He tried

again and Sheila said, "Keep that up and you'll be back asleep. Is that what you want?"

"No. What I want is a cigarette."

"Sorry. No smoking."

In the darkness, Remo could see the outline of some large box on the back of the boat.

"Over here," she said, steering Remo. As he got closer, he saw the box was an iron-barred cage, almost the size of a side-by-side, washer-dryer combination. Piled on top of it were black drapes. With her free hand, Sheila opened the door of the cage and pushed Remo toward it.

"In there."

"Is this really necessary?" Remo asked.

"I can't spend my time worrying about you trying to hop overboard. Get in."

"And if I say no?"

"Then I'll put you in anyway," Sheila said. "I'm really very strong, you know."

Even in the dark, her teeth and eyes glinted, picking up the faint glow of faraway lights and turning them into sharp, shining dagger beams.

Remo decided to try it. He yanked his arm away, this time spinning his body while he did it, to put the full force of his weight behind the move. It was the kind of move he knew so well. He never thought about it before. But now he found it necessary to plot each step as he did it. Muscle memory, the ability of the body to do routine tasks without the brain being called in to direct, had deserted him. It was this skill that characterized and united the great athlete, the great typist, and the great seamstress. Memory of what the body must do was stamped into the muscles and bypassed the brain.

He smiled to himself as it worked. As his body spun, he felt his arm slip from Sheila Feinberg's hand. He was free. But his back was toward her and that was something the art of Sinanju warned against. Be-

146

fore he could remember and move away, Sheila was on his back. Remo felt strong hands around his throat, pressing, searching for the arteries in his neck. Then he felt the pulse throbbing heavily in his throat as the blood flow to his brain closed off. Darkness spread into his head.

Remo dropped heavily onto the deck of the boat. He could feel his body hit as his eyes closed but then was done. He did not feel Sheila push him into the cage, lock the door with a padlock, then drape the sides with the thick black curtains.

As Remo slept, the boat started and Sheila sped away, leaving behind the big boat she had used to escape from Folcroft, leaving it to drift aimlessly with the current through Long Island Sound.

She turned due east and gave the boat full throttle. She roared through the night for the ninety-minute run to Bridgeport.

Remo woke again when the boat stopped. He felt Sheila Feinberg's hands reach through the bars of the cage and clamp around his throat.

She hissed. "Now, we can do this easy or we can do it hard. Easy is, you just be quiet and you can stay awake. Hard is, you make a sound and I put you back to sleep. But if I have to do it again, I'm going to leave you with some new scars."

Remo opted for easy. Maybe if he caused her no trouble, she'd give him what he really wanted in life.

A cigarette.

Then a steak. Rare, with juice running out, the kind called black-and-blue he had once gotten in a restaurant in Weehawken, New Jersey.

Remo remembered that steak for a moment, savoring its taste in his mind. Then he remembered where he was and who he was with and the idea of rare meat made him shudder.

Chiun supervised as Smith removed the bodies

147

from the hallway outside Remo's room, then went to his own room, refusing to talk to Smith. Smith was too busy to talk anyway. He went directly to his office.

Smith's name was unknown in any government circle. In no Washington office did a picture of him hang on the wall, a photographic offering to protect the owner from lightning, flood and firing.

But in his anonymous way, he commanded more powerful armies than any other man in America. More of the levers that turned the wheels of government were brought together in his office than anywhere else. Thousands of people were on his direct payroll. Thousands of others worked for other agencies, but their reports came to CURE, even though not one of them knew it and none would have obeyed a direct order from Smith if it had been hand-delivered by a marine regiment.

The young president who had chosen Smith to head the secret organization, CURE, had selected wisely. He had picked a man to whom personal prestige and power meant nothing. He was interested only in enough power to do his job well. His character was constructed in such a way that he would never abuse that power.

Now Smith was using that power.

In minutes, military helicopters were crisscrossing Long Island Sound looking for a twenty-seven-foot Silverton with a Bimini bridge.

Federal agents were soon watching bridges, tunnels and toll booths between Rye, New York, and Boston, Massachusetts. They had been told they were looking for a diplomat who had been abducted after being granted asylum in the United States. His name was secret but he had dark hair and eyes, high cheekbones, and very thick wrists. The rest was very hush–hush.

Airport security forces and maritime inspectors at

seaports all over the East were put on the alert for the same kind of man. All they knew was that it was important to find him.

After putting all those forces to work, Smith sat in his office to wait. He spun his chair around, looking out at the waters of Long Island Sound. He was not too confident because government was like the water at which he stared. The water's action could be predicted, because its ebb and flow was on its own schedule and its own clock. But control it?

It was that way with government. Sometimes you could predict its flow but only a fool believed he could control it. Just as the waters of the Sound. They had come and gone for hundreds and thousands of years. Hundreds and thousands of years from now, someone else would be sitting in Smith's chair, looking out at the waters. They would still be moving in their own rhythm, in their own time.

The telephone rang. It was the wrong phone and wasn't the call for which Smith had hoped.

"Yes, Mr. President," he said.

"I didn't think I'd be making any more calls to you," the President said, "but just what the hell is going on?"

"What do you mean, sir?" Smith asked.

"I'm getting reports. It seems like this whole peckerheaded government has gone on some kind of alert. Are you responsible for that?"

"Yes, sir, I am."

"Why, when you're supposed to be doing something about that Boston mess?"

"This is part of that Boston mess, as you put it," said Smith.

"I thought your secret weapon would have resolved all that by now anyway." There was sarcasm in the President's soft, honey-coated voice.

"That secret weapon has been injured and cap-

149

tured, sir," Smith said. "It is important that he be found before—"

"Before he talks?" the President interrupted.

"Yes. Or before he is killed."

The President sighed. "If he talks, he brings down the government. Not just my administration, but the entire concept of constitutional government. I guess you know that."

"I know that, sir."

"How can we stop him from talking?"

"By locating him."

"And then what?"

"If there is any danger of his revealing what he should not, I will handle it," Smith said.

"How?" asked the President.

"I don't think you'd want to know the answer to that, Mr. President," said Smith.

The President, who understood full well that he had just heard a man promise to kill another if it became necessary for the country's best interests, said softly, "Oh. I'll leave it with you."

"That would be best. We have destroyed some of the Boston creatures. That should reduce the death toll there."

"Cutting back is small consolation. I don't think the American people are going to be comforted if I tell them we've managed to cut the murder rate from mutated people by sixty-seven percent. From six a day to two a day."

"No, sir, I guess not. We are continuing to work on it," Smith said.

"Good night," the President said. "When this is all over, assuming we survive, I think I would like to meet you."

"Good night, sir," Smith said noncommittally.

The next call was the one Smith wanted. A Coast Guard official, who thought he was talking to an FBI agent for Westchester County, reported a helicopter had found a twenty-nine-foot Silverton. It was empty and drifting through the Sound without lights. There was no one aboard.

The owner was a New Jersey dentist who said he had sold the boat only eight hours earlier for twenty-seven thousand dollars. Cash. The buyer was a young man who wore a gold sunburst medallion around his neck.

Smith thanked the man and hung up.

That was that. A dead end. The man with the sunburst medallion had been one of the tiger people. Smith had shot him in the upstairs hallway outside Remo's room. That trail was cold and dead.

Smith waited at his telephone for the rest of the night but it did not ring again.

CHAPTER THIRTEEN

It was still night when the small jet landed on a bumpy runway. After the plane had come to a full stop, Remo felt his cage being dragged to the cargo door, then dumped five feet to the ground.

"Hey, goddammit, that hurt," Remo yelled. His voice echoed inside the cage, rebounding off the heavy black drapes.

Then all was still until he heard the plane's motors start up again. The sound seemed to be right above his ears. At one time he had been able to block out noises, closing his ears the way other persons could close their eyes, but he could not do it now.

The screeching wail of the engines continued, reverberating over his head, setting his teeth on edge, growing ever louder. Then, mercifully, he could hear the plane move away, lurching along the runway, its motors burned to full power. Remo could hear the plane taking off, vanishing in the distance.

The night was still, except for the creaking of insects, who sounded as if they were holding a quorum call of all the bugs that ever lived.

Remo wished he had a cigarette. The side curtain was lifted and tossed on top of the cage. Sheila Feinberg stood there, outside the bars, wearing shorts that barely covered her crotch and a matching khaki top stretched taut over her enormous breasts.

"How are you doing?" she asked.

"Fine," Remo said through the bars. "Time really flies when you're having fun."

"Do you want to get out of there?"

"Either that or send me maid service. Whatever makes you happy."

Sheila leaned on the bars of the cage.

"Look. I think you know by now I can take you. If you remember that and don't mess around trying to escape, I'll let you out. But if you're going to be difficult you can stay in the cage. Your choice."

"Let me out," Remo said.

"All right. That's better all around," Sheila said.

She fished a key from the pocket of her shorts, which Remo thought were too tight to allow the intromission of anything, and unlocked the padlock on the cage.

Remo crawled onto the chipped and broken blacktop of the runway, rose to his feet, and stretched. "That feels good," he said.

"All right. Let's go," Sheila said. She led the way to a jeep that was parked alongside the runway. Remo got into the passenger's side as she started the motor.

"One thing," Remo said. "You are Sheila Feinberg, aren't you?"

"That's right."

"Your photographs don't do you justice," he said.

"My pictures are of what I used to look like. That was a long time ago."

Remo nodded. "And where are we?"

"Dominican Republic. Eighteen miles outside of Santo Domingo."

"You've brought me a long way just to kill me."

"Who's going to kill you?" asked Sheila. "I've got other plans for you." She turned to Remo and smiled, a smile full of teeth that did not make Remo feel at all good.

"What plans?" Remo asked.

"You're going into stud service," she said, and laughed aloud as she drove away from the runway onto a narrow dirt road, leading toward rolling hills a half-dozen miles away.

Remo sat back to enjoy the ride, if he could. He still wished he had a cigarette.

They stopped at a white farmhouse on the edge of a sugar cane field, the size of four, square, city blocks. The sugar had long ago been harvested. Most of the cane was cut and gone.

Only little patches remained, sitting in the field like random tufts of hair on a bald man. The cut husks were dry. When Remo stepped on one, it crackled under his foot as if he had jumped into a pail of cellophane.

The house was clean and well provisioned. A noisy gasoline generator outside provided electricity to run the lights and the refrigerator. The first thing Remo looked for and found were cigarettes in a cupboard in the kitchen. He lit one quickly and savored the taste of smoke rolling over his tongue, depositing droplets of tar onto his teeth, gums, and tongue on its poisonous way into his lungs.

The second thing he looked for and found was a package of Twinkies in the refrigerator. He ripped open the cellophane with his teeth and shoved the cake into his mouth. Two of life's great pleasures, he thought. A cigarette and a chocolate-flavored lump of refined sugar.

It hadn't been long ago that his diet was rice, fish,

155

duck, and occasionally vegetables. How long had it been since he'd had something sweet? How had he gone without for all those years?

Remo had a second Twinkie in his mouth when Sheila appeared in the doorway of the kitchen. She had changed into a gauzy white robe that left none of her body to the imagination but instead offered it to Remo as a gift. She opened her mouth to say something, then clamped it tight, brushed past Remo and violently stubbed out his cigarette in the ashtray.

"Hey, I was smoking that," he said.

"It's about time you learned smoking is bad for your health," she said. She turned to him again and brushed her breasts against his chest. "On the other hand, I might be very good for your health."

Remo, Twinkie in hand, felt something else he hadn't felt in many years—desire, burning, sexual desire for a woman. The art of Sinanju had made him a user of women's bodies when he wanted to be; it had taught him techniques to send women up walls in frenzy. But in making it an art and a science, Sinanju had made it dull. Remo couldn't remember the last time he had been aroused.

Till now.

He stuffed the rest of the Twinkie in his mouth and put his arms around Sheila Feinberg. His bodily urges made his mind not care that the woman had ripped open his stomach and throat only a few weeks before.

He ran his hands down her slick back, feeling the tightness of smooth flesh through the flimsy nylon. Then he placed his hands on the rounded globes of her behind, pulling her to him and feeling, with pleasure, his body responding.

She raised her mouth to his and he covered it with his lips.

Then Sheila Feinberg lifted and carried him into the bedroom where she placed him gently on the bed.

"Does this mean we're going together?" Remo asked.

Sheila took off her wrap and lay on the bed next to him. "You're here to provide stud services," she said. "Now provide."

Remo did. For a full thirty seconds.

The same art that had killed desire was itself killed when desire returned. It was over before he realized it. He felt embarrassed at his lack of control.

"You're not much," Sheila said with a thin pursing of her lips.

"I'll get better," he said.

"You'll have plenty of practice," she said. Coldly, with no afterglow from the sex act, she rose from the bed and walked out the door. Remo heard it lock behind her.

"Go to sleep," she called through the door. "You'll need your rest."

Remo did not mind. He had put the pack of cigarettes in his trouser pocket before leaving the kitchen. Now he fished them out, lit one and lay back on the bed smoking, flicking ashes on the floor and considering that life was all a matter of timing.

Ten, thirteen years ago, before he joined CURE, he could think of few things better than being the captive love slave of a voluptuous blonde whose only demand was that he screw well and often. Now here he was, and all he felt was uncomfortable.

He smoked three cigarettes, stubbed them out on the floor, kicked the butts under the bed, and fell asleep. He slept hard and loglike. When he woke in the morning the bedroom door had been unlocked and left ajar.

Sheila stood naked at the kitchen sink, her body glowing with health and strength, an X-rated display of centerfold perfection.

"Do you want to make it before or after you eat?" she asked when Remo came in.

157

"After."

Remo saw the food on his plate. Uncooked bacon and a bowl of raw eggs.

"Before," he amended.

"After," she said.

"This stuff isn't cooked," Remo said.

"I didn't want to fool with that stove," Sheila said.

"Who can eat this?" Remo asked, but saw that Sheila had sat down at the table and was eating it, dropping the strips of fatted, slick, white bacon down her throat like a finalist in a goldfish swallowing exhibition.

"I've done the best I can," Sheila said sharply. "If you don't like my breakfast, too bad. Eat cereal."

"I'll cook this," Remo said, lifting up his plate and bowl.

"You'll leave that stove alone. Eat cereal," Sheila said.

Remo had a Twinkie. When he was done, Sheila put a strong hand on his shoulder and led him into the bedroom.

"Come on, Ace," she said. "We'll see if we can get you up to the full minute mark today."

Remo followed, wondering dully what it was all about, but deciding not to worry. At least not until the cigarettes were gone.

It was the third day at Folcroft. Autopsies had been performed on the three tiger people killed and the results confirmed Smith's worst fears. The three had undergone chromosomal change. They were, in point of fact, no longer human beings. They were something else, something between man and beast. Smith worried that the thing they had become might turn out to be stronger and smarter, even more bloodthirsty than man.

The deaths in Boston continued but their number declined. It might have been the presence of the National Guard patrolling the streets. More likely, Smith felt, it was that he had decimated the tiger people's forces with the three deaths. That meant Sheila Feinberg—Smith was now convinced it was she who had carried Remo off—had not gone back to Boston. If she had, she would have by now created more maneaters. The toll would have begun climbing again.

There was another thought gnawing at Smith, a thought at once so frightening and painful that he consciously tried to put it out of his mind. Yet it persisted. Suppose Sheila Feinberg had taken Remo to make him one of them? Remo, with all his skills, but coupled with brainless, animal savagery? He had been unstoppable before and now would be worse, therefore must be stopped. In those circumstances, there was only one man in the world who could stop him.

But how could Smith raise the subject?

Smith tapped lightly on the door of the second floor room. There was no answer. He pushed the door open and stepped inside.

Chiun wore a white purification robe and sat on a grass mat in the center of the floor. The room's two windows were heavily draped. Candles flickered at the four corners of the darkened room, which was bare of furniture. In front of Chiun, incense burned in a small porcelain bowl.

"Chiun?" Smith said softly.

"Yes."

"I'm sorry. There's been no word on Remo. He and that woman seem to have vanished off the face of the earth."

"He is dead," Chiun intoned dully.

"How can you be so sure?"

"Because I wish it so," Chiun said after a pause.

"You? Wish it so? Why, for God's sake?"

"Because if Remo is not dead, he will become one of them. If he becomes one of them, one hundred

159

generations of Masters of Sinanju will demand I send him home to the sea. Even if he is my son. Because I have taught and given him Sinanju I may never permit it to be misused. So, because I do not wish to . . ." Chiun could not bring himself to say the word "kill." ". . . because I do not wish to remove him, I wish him to be already dead."

"I understand," Smith said. His question had already been answered. If Remo was changed, Chiun would dispose of him. He began to say "thank you" to Chiun but caught himself.

The old man's head had sunk low again on his chest. Smith knew there was no conversation left in him. He wondered how many more days the death rites of Sinanju must continue.

Remo had a good guess now why Adam and Eve made a deal with the devil to get out of paradise. It was too damned dull.

Six days. The weather was always perfect. Sheila Feinberg was always beautiful and available.

Remo had to do nothing but lounge around the farmhouse and perform when Sheila wanted him to.

He was bored.

To make matters worse, he had run out of Twinkies and was running low on cigarettes. The cigarettes might have lasted but Sheila had this annoying habit of running around and, whenever she saw a cigarette, jabbing it out in the ash tray.

Nor did she put it out like a civilized person, just squashing the end so later Remo could salvage the clincher and smoke what was left. No, she jabbed cigarettes out with as much power as if she were throwing darts and usually managed to bust them in at least two places. There was no way to smoke the butts later on. She also kept throwing away his matches which he had now taken to hiding under his mattress.

The food was nothing to speak of either. Sheila refused to allow the stove to be used. She would sit, eating raw meat in her bare hands, blood running down the sides of her mouth. When she was done she would lick her red fingers and eye Remo as if he were 165 pounds of ambulatory filet mignon.

Remo subsisted on package food and cake. He began to remember the good old days when the paddies were filled with rice for the world and the oceans were abundant and swollen with fish. But he did not miss rice and fish all that much.

He wondered occasionally about Chiun and whether he would ever see him again. Probably Chiun already had forgotten about him and was looking for somebody else to train. Well, Remo could live with that. He had had enough of training and bitching. He had had enough too of Smith and all those hours of work trying to do everything and be every place. Enough. Enough. Enough.

Remo went out to the porch surrounding the white farmhouse. There was a three-foot-high wooden railing along the front. Remo leaned on it with his hands. He remembered how Chiun trained him by making him run along narrow railings to improve his balance. Remo had run across cables on the Golden Gate Bridge, run along the top of deck railings on ocean liners in choppy seas. A porch railing? A breeze. Remo removed his hands from the railing and hopped into the air. As his feet came down on the railing, his right foot slipped. He hit his knee a sharp crack on the way down.

He was puzzled at that. He didn't usually slip. He jumped up again. This time he made it, but teetered, rocking back and forth, trying not to fall off. He extended his arms far out to the sides, curled his body like a ball and swayed back and forth, trying to stay on the railing.

"You really are a mess."

When Sheila's voice came from behind, Remo lost his concentration. Before tumbling forward into a bush, he pushed himself backward and jumped heavily to the aged, wooden floor of the porch.

"What do you mean by that?" Remo asked as he turned. Sheila stood in the doorway, naked as usual. It made it easier for them to couple at random moments.

"When I first ran into you, you were something exceptional. That's why you're here," she said. "And now? Just another young, out of shape nothing. With enough years, you might grow up to be an old, out-of-shape nothing."

She did not try to mask the contempt she felt for him.

"Wait a minute. What do you mean that's why I'm here?" Remo asked.

She smiled. "That's another thing. Your brain doesn't work either. If you can't figure it out, don't expect me to tell you. Come in and eat your breakfast. You need your strength."

"I'm tired of cereal and Twinkies," Remo said.

"Suits me. Eat grass."

Sheila walked back inside the house. When she and Remo first arrived, she watched him at all times to prevent his escaping. If he was not being watched, he was kept locked up. But now she ignored him, as if she had gauged his physical condition and decided there was no way he would be able to escape.

He wondered if he had really fallen that far. That a woman treated him with physical contempt? What good was Sinanju if it deserted you that quickly?

Or had he deserted it?

He leaned back against the railing and again felt the wood under his fingertips. Only a few weeks ago, he could have told in the dark what kind of wood it was, how dry, how old, how slippery it might be when

162

wet and exactly what force might be needed to break it.

But now it was just a piece of wood, senseless, dead wood. It told him no story.

He had turned his back on Sinanju so it had turned its back on him. He had stopped the training, forgotten how to breathe, forgotten how to make his body something different from other men's bodies.

He had turned his back on other things too. What of Chiun who had for years been more father than father could be? Who had taught him out of love the wisdom of centuries of Sinanju? What of Smith and the mind-breaking tensions he worked under? His need to solve the tiger people problem in Boston? The pressure from the President?

Remo realized he had walked away from his only family, his only friends. In doing that he had walked away from the art of Sinanju which had made him, for better or for worse, what he was.

Remo paused and looked around the porch. He took a deep breath. The air was fresh and clean. He breathed again, reaching down deep, filling his lungs, then pulling the breath all the way into the pit of his groin as he had learned day after day, month after month, year after year.

Like a sluice gate being opened in flood time, the air poured through and triggered memories of what he once had been. He could taste the air as well as smell it. There was the sweetness of sugar and the rotten smell of decaying vegetation. There was humidity in the breath. He could smell the sea nearby, almost taste the salt, and there was a breeze coming from over the mountains.

He breathed again and could smell the animals of the fields. He could smell the meat from Sheila's kitchen table, the rotten sweet, flesh smell of dead meat. He could smell the dryness of the boards under his feet. It was as if he had been dead and was alive again.

Remo laughed aloud as life poured in through his senses. Sinanju was an art of death but to its practitioners, it brought only life, life being lived to its fullest, every sense alive and vibrant with feeling and power.

Remo laughed again. The porch rocked with the sound. Laughter bounced off the front wall of the house.

He turned and leaped high into the air.

He came down lightly with both feet on the narrow wooden railing. He stood motionless, his body as firmly balanced as if he had been rooted in the wood.

With his eyes closed, he jumped in the air, spun and came down with both feet, one behind the other, facing in the opposite direction. He ran forward along the railing then back, keeping his eyes closed, sensing the thickness of the wood through the soles of his feet, letting the power of nature flow from the wood into his body.

And he laughed again. It was over.

Inside, Sheila Feinberg did not hear him. She had just finished her breakfast of raw, bloody beef liver. She sat at the table and threw it back up onto her plate.

She looked at her vomit and smiled. The part of her that was animal had been giving her signals for thirty-six hours. Now the part that was woman seemed to be giving a signal. If it was the signal she had been looking for, she would have no more use for Remo.

Except as a meal.

On the porch, Remo took the pack of cigarettes from his trouser pocket, crushed it in his hand, and threw it toward the field of cut cane. He had no more use for cigarettes.

But he kept the matches.

CHAPTER FOURTEEN

It wasn't so much that the lady bartender at the Three Musketeers was beautiful, which she was, but that she had not seemed impressed by Durwood Dawkins. His Cadillac hadn't impressed her, nor had the large wad of bills he usually carried. But, she seemed to be impressed by the fact that he was a jet pilot for hire. Maybe, possibly, would he take her for a ride someday?

"Sure," he said, "Any day or night." Then he impressed her some more by telling her how quickly they could get to so many different places. Why, just last week it had taken only three hours to fly a private party to the Dominican Republic. And what a strange party. A great-looking blonde in short shorts accompanied by a cage. The cage, he knew, had a man in it because he heard him yell when the cage was dropped from the plane's cargo door.

These things did Durwood Dawkins tell the bartender. Because he had already had four martinis, he

165

told most of the rest of the bar, too, including a man at the end who wore old gray chinos and threadbare shirts and had been able to support his terminally ill wife and family for the past four years only because he made a phone call once a week to pass on anything interesting he had heard. He made this call for $45 a week. The person he called told him only two days ago they were looking for a blonde woman and a dark-haired man with thick wrists.

Big Mouth Dawkins' story might not mean anything but then again it might. The man with the chinos finished the one beer he allowed himself on his way home from work every night and called that special telephone number. Perhaps this time there might even be a bonus.

An hour later, the lady bartender was getting ready to go off duty. Durwood Dawkins wished his apartment was cleaner. It would make for a neater score. But while she was in the back checking out, Dawkins was met at the bar by a man with a voice so dry it sounded as if his throat were lined with graham crackers.

"Are you Durwood Dawkins, the pilot?" the man asked.

Dawkins sized the man up quickly. He didn't look like much. An old suit. Unstyled hair. He wasn't a client or an owner. It was therefore safe to be rude.

"Who wants to know?"

"My name is Smith. Tell me about your flight last week to the islands."

"What flight?"

"The blonde woman. The cage with the man in it."

"Who told you about that?" Dawkins asked.

"That doesn't matter. I know about it," Smith said.

"Well, I don't feel like talking about it." Dawkins looked around to see if anyone was watching. The blonde woman with the cage had paid him extra well to keep his mouth closed. While there wasn't a chance in hell she'd get any of her money back, if she complained, word could get around that Dawkins wasn't as closemouthed as he should be. That might cut into business a little too much for comfort.

"I'm sorry. You'll just have to talk about that," said Smith.

"Are you threatening me?" asked Dawkins. Despite best intentions, his voice got louder. Martini volume.

"No. I'm trying to avoid that," Smith said, lowering his voice to counter Dawkins' increased volume. "I won't tell you that if I want, you will have no pilot's license in the morning. I won't discuss the regular trips you make to Mexico and the unusual cargo you carry out. In little paper bags. I'd rather not get into those things. What I want to know is whom did you fly. Where did you set them down? Who paid you? Who were the passengers? Did they say anything?"

With alcohol-induced bravery, Durwood Dawkins refused to be intimidated, although his stomach did an Immelmann loop confronted with knowledge of his little drug-running trips from Mexico.

"You want answers, ask Dear Abby," he said. "She answers questions. I don't."

Forgotten now was the lady bartender changing her clothes in the back room. Dawkins said, "I'm leaving."

"Have it your own way," Smith said. "You would have done better to answer in here."

"Leave me alone," Dawkins said. Smith reached out to touch the man's shoulder. Dawkins pulled away before the older man could touch him and stomp toward the door.

The relief bartender asked Smith, "What can I get you, sir?"

"Nothing, thank you. I don't drink."

Smith took a pack of matches and a free pretzel

167

from the bar. He followed Dawkins outside. As he neared the door there was a muted yell.

When he got to the sidewalk, Durwood Dawkins had just completed a merger with a parking meter.

His body was on the sidewalk side of the meter but his right hand had gone through the top of the meter. His fingers fluttered around on the street side of the instrument.

Chiun stood alongside him.

"He is ready to talk to you now, Emperor."

Smith cleared his throat. He stood so that his body shielded Dawkins' wildly fluttering hand from the view of passers-by.

"Now. Who and where and when and what?" he asked.

"I want my hand free first," Dawkins said.

"Where would you like it?" asked Chiun, moving close. "I can put it in your left pocket. I can leave it in the trunk of your car. If the emperor wishes, we can mail it to you. It is for you to decide, big-mouthed one."

"First I'll talk," said Dawkins to Smith. The pilot's eyes rolled in terror. But you've got to promise to keep this guy off me," he told Smith.

"Just talk," Smith said.

Five minutes later, Smith and Chiun were heading for a helicopter which would take them to Westchester Country Airport, where a private jet was waiting. Next stop: the Dominican Republic.

And 1500 miles away in the Dominican Republic, Sheila Feinberg threw up her lunch, great chunks of raw steak that had stayed in her stomach only long enough for gastric juices to discolor the red a sickly greenish-gray.

She laughed. The part of her that was tiger had told her before, but now the woman part confirmed it. It was morning sickness.

She was pregnant. With the first baby of a new species.

Remo had done what he was designed to do and now, frankly, she found him a little tiresome. It was time to get rid of him.

Maybe she would be able to keep *that* meal down.

CHAPTER FIFTEEN

"Remo, where are you? It's time again."

She was moving toward him but it was somehow different. Remo felt her motion through the floor-boards of the old farmhouse, but she wasn't walking as she normally walked. Her movements were slow, deliberate, as if she were looking for the right spots to place her feet. Remo knew it for what it was. It signalled lie at her come-on-and-have-sex words.

She was stalking him. The time had come.

Remo hopped lightly over the porch railing and ran into the farmland in front of the house. New cane had started to grow, interspersed with high, thick, stringy weed. There were tufts of vegetation where Remo could take shelter and be unseen.

He ran through a half dozen of them, scraping his feet, rubbing himself against the weeds, then moved far off to the edge of the field and waited.

He heard Sheila's voice again.

"Where are you, bad boy?" she called. "Come to Mama."

The comic-book attempt to be seductive was out of character. Another time, Remo might have laughed aloud. But not now. She would be after him in a moment, and Remo wondered just how good he still was. Had he gotten back enough of Sinanju?

She had almost killed him once before when he was at the peak of his powers. What now when he was out of training and out of shape?

Sheila was on the porch. Remo could see her by peering around the edge of a clump of weeds.

She was naked. Her hands were in front of her, over her head, her fingers curled like claws. She stopped on the porch and turned her head to the left, then to the right.

She was sniffing the air. Then she caught Remo's scent leading to the cane field. From her throat came an angry, violent roar, a tiger's roar the ferocity of which freezes prey in their tracks, rooting them to the ground with fear.

She came off the porch, her hands back at her sides, her head bent low, smelling Remo's scent.

"You know, you can't get away," she yelled out. "Your trying to is just going to make it easier to eat you."

She moved along the line of Remo's scent, trotting briskly, moving so quickly it was as if she was following a paved path through the field.

Remo crouched low, keeping out of sight. He ran toward the house. He felt the breeze touch the right side of his body and knew his fresh scent was not being carried toward her.

At the side of the house, he found the gasoline generator that powered the house's lights and refrigerator. There were two full five-gallon, gasoline cans.

Remo grabbed one in each hand and began to retrace his path to the field.

Sheila was still calling him. Her voice echoed in the still day with an almost inhuman volume.

She paused at the first clump of bushes where Remo had left his scent and sniffed around it.

"How did you guess," she called, "that your work here was done?" She straightened up and began following Remo's old path through the field. "No use hopping around," she called. "You can't hide from me."

As she reached the second cluster of greenery where Remo had paused, she said, "It's sort of a shame, isn't it, that you won't be around to see the race you helped create?"

Remo was pouring gasoline along the path he had followed near the far side of the field. Staying low, one gas can on its side under his arm, he ran along. The gas spilled out splashing bushes and dead, dry grass.

It took one full can and more than half the other. By the time Sheila had reached the sixth cluster of cane and weed Remo had scented, he had finished circling the field with gasoline and was back near the porch of the house.

He was out of shape. He could feel it. The ripped stomach muscles had knitted and the skin had healed without much of a scar, but muscle tone had deteriorated. He could feel strain from having run with the two five-gallon cans under his arms. Remo dropped the cans and shrugged.

He could see Sheila rising from the crouch where she had been sniffing his trail around the sixth cluster of bushes he had reached. Before she could follow him back to the house, Remo dashed forward into the center of the field and called out, "Hey, pussycat, where are you?"

Sheila stood up tall, a growl rumbling deep in her

throat. She saw Remo and smiled, a broad predator's smile, that expressed neither happiness nor joy, merely satisfaction over finding the next meal so neatly served.

She moved toward him slowly, body bent from the waist, her full and shapely breasts pointing toward the ground, their tips hardened with a passion that had nothing to do with sex. They seemed smaller than they had been.

"I thought you'd give me a better chase than this," she said.

"It's too hot to play," Remo said.

"Even with the mother of your child?" Sheila asked.

The words hit Remo like a hammer, triggering years of frustrated knowledge that he would never have a home, never have children, never have a place of his own that he didn't have to pay for by the night.

"What do you mean?" he said.

"I'm carrying your baby. That's what you were here for, stupid." Sheila was only twenty yards from him now.

"Why?"

"Because I'm going to make more and more of my new people. Someday my son will lead them. He'll have the world."

It wasn't his baby, Remo thought. A baby was made by love between two people. Two humans. This thing, if it existed, would be a grotesque mimicry of an infant, half human, half animal, a snarling vicious beast of a killer.

If he ever had a baby with those traits, he wanted them to come from him, not from its mother. In that moment, for the first time, he hated Sheila Feinberg, hated her for the mockery she had made of his fatherhood, using him as a stud horse, not knowing or caring how much a child would mean to Remo.

In his anger Remo called back, "Have the world? He'll sleep in a tree, eat scraps from the butcher shop

174

and be lucky if he doesn't spend his days in a zoo. With you, you half-witted, half-breed, half-assed alley cat."

Sheila shivered with anger. "I might even have kept you alive," she said. "But you just don't understand. I'm the new breed of man."

"You're the same old breed of lunatic," Remo said.

She was ten yards from him now and charged, fingers raised over her head, head tilted toward the side, mouth open and long, white teeth glistening with saliva.

Her speed surprised Remo, she was almost on him before he could react. Just as she closed the space between them, Remo ducked low, rolled on the ground to the left and came up running.

Sheila's charge missed Remo and carried her forward into the bushes. She pulled herself back and ran after Remo.

Remo knew. He was far from what he had been. He had hoped he was 100 percent, but he wasn't even 50. Sheila was an animal at the peak of her strength, in the prime of her power and youth.

But Remo had something else. He had man's intelligence. It was that intelligence that enabled man to conquer the world by using the bestial instincts of animals as weapons against those same animals.

He reached the edge of the field, and turned to face Sheila's charge. He pulled the book of matches from his back pocket and waited. When she reached him she feinted left, then came right. He could feel her long nails rake down his left shoulder and knew he was bleeding. At the same time, he went down, under her body, and came up into the pit of her stomach with the stiffened heel of the hand.

"Ooooof," she hissed as the air rushed out of her body.

He had missed. The blow would have killed if he had been on target. Sheila hit the ground, rolled to her feet, and spun to face Remo. Her glistening white skin was now caked with dirt and bits of dried grass. She looked like an animal that had taken a mud bath, then rolled in straw.

Before she could charge again, Remo struck a match and threw it past her. It landed in the gasoline line Remo had spilled and erupted into flame with a whoosh. The dried cane and weeds crackled. Like a fuse lit in the center, the fire sped in both directions circling the two fighters in the field.

Sheila's eyes widened with fear and shock. Remo knew he had been right. Of all animals on earth, only man had conquered the fire fear. Her stubbing out of cigarettes, her refusal to use a simple, kitchen stove, had told him Sheila too feared the flame.

She jumped away from the fire crackling behind her. Now she was in a pocket, surrounded on three sides by flames with Remo standing in front of her.

She charged him again and Remo executed a slow rolling movement of his upper body that carried her by him. As he tried to back off again toward the flames, he was too slow. She slapped out a hand. It caught his ankle and tripped him into the dirt. Then she was on him. Remo could feel her weight on his back, her claws trying to tear out his neck.

Without panic, knowing what he was doing, Remo scurried forward, carrying Sheila Feinberg on his back. When he reached the ring of fire, she dropped off and fell away from him. Her eyes glistened with hatred as she faced him over a distance of only ten feet.

"That fire won't burn forever," she hissed. "Then you'll die. You can't keep running from me."

"Don't jump to conclusions," Remo said. "That's the trouble with you cats, always jumping to conclusions. Now *I'm* going to attack."

Remo had taken Sheila's three charges and knew the pattern now. She came in with arms raised, head tilted, belly an open invitation to attack. It was time to accept that invitation before she wore him down.

Remo darted out of the little cul-de-sac of flame, moving around Sheila, circling her, until there was no flame directly behind him and she felt safe to charge.

She came in again, arms raised, head tilted. As she neared, Remo went to the ground and came up with the heels of both feet, burying them deep into her soft white belly.

Sheila went into the air with the thrust of Remo's legs, turning a lazy half-sommersault. Like a cat, she twisted her body on the way to earth, to land on her feet.

Instead she landed on a spike of cut sugar cane, which, like a spear, buried itself in Sheila Feinberg's stomach.

Almost in slow motion, as Remo watched, her body slid down the bamboolike spike. It exited from her back, bloodied, raw bits of flesh stuck to it.

She was dying and looked at him with not pain but bewilderment, the look unreasoning animals get when they encounter the reality of their own death.

Remo rolled to his feet and walked toward Sheila Feinberg.

She gestured to him with a hand, moving jerkily, like a pantomimist aping a robot.

"I've got to tell you something," she hissed. "Come here."

Remo knelt near Sheila to listen. As he did her teeth opened wide and she drove her mouth toward his open throat. But she was slow now. With the passing of life had gone her speed. Remo just leaned back and her teeth closed harmlessly on air. Her face fell back down into the dirt.

Remo stood and looked down as she breathed her last.

"Sorry, but that's the biz, sweetheart," he said.

Suddenly he felt fatigue wash over his body, like a

giant wave engulfing a swimmer. He wanted to sleep, to rest, and when he awakened, to rededicate his body to Sinanju. But there was something he had to do first, or there would never be any rest for him.

The flames had died but the field still smoldered when Chiun and Smith arrived a few minutes later in the rented jeep that had met them at the airport. The rental agent for the jeeps on the island had remembered well the blonde woman with the cage and instructions to the farmhouse were simple and direct.

Remo was standing in the field, his back to them, as they approached.

The naked body of Sheila Feinberg lay on its back on the ground in front of him. The gash in her stomach had opened even wider, and when Remo turned to them, Smith saw his hands were red with blood.

Remo smiled when he saw Chiun.

"Are you all right?" Smith asked.

"I'm fine. She wasn't pregnant," Remo said and walked back to the farmhouse to wash.

Chiun walked along behind him, matching him step for step.

"Look at you," he said. "Fat. You're fat. Fat, fat, fat."

"I know, Little Father," Remo said. "I've learned something."

"It will be the first time. And do you know how much I spent on candles for you?"

Remo stopped and looked at Chiun. "Doing death rituals? I know something about Sinanju, Little Father. I know that's only for blood of your own blood."

"Your life was so worthless, I thought I would ennoble your death," said Chiun, peevishly. "Then you went and didn't die on me. All those candles are ruined."

"We'll get you some more," Remo said. "You know,

178

Chiun, even though I'm not much, you're lucky to have me as a son. It must be good to have a son."

"It's good to have a good son," Chiun said. "But one like you is like no son at all. Really, Remo, you have no consideration at all."

"Fat, too. Don't forget that."

When Remo came out of the farmhouse, Smith had just finished inspecting the woman's body.

"Was this Sheila Feinberg?" he asked.

"That's her," said Remo.

Smith nodded. "Well, at least she won't be making any more tiger people. Did you, by any chance, find out the names of any of the ones still in Boston?"

"No," said Remo.

"Well, when you go back there, I guess you can clean them up kind of quickly. Especially now that you know how they behave."

"I'm not going back there, Smitty," Remo said.

"But they're still there. Still killing," Smith said.

"They'll stop soon. They're almost done."

"You sound sure," Smith said.

"I am. I told you, she wasn't pregnant."

Remo would say no more. He was silent riding in the jeep to the airstrip where Smith's private jet waited for them.

In the plane, Chiun spoke to him softly.

"She was changing back, wasn't she?" he said.

Remo nodded. "How did you know?"

"Her body. It had lost its grace. That thing could not move like the thing that took you from the sanitarium last week."

"You're right, Little Father," Remo said. "She had been throwing up her meals. She thought it was morning sickness and pregnancy. But it wasn't. It was her body rejecting the change. Her shape was changing too and she was losing strength. She was on her way back."

179

"So the others in Boston, they will change back too," Chiun said.

"That's right. So I guess we can just leave them alone."

Smith joined them as Chiun said, "Still it was not a bad attempt. If we could make it permanent, we could get some of this NDA . . ."

"DNA," said Smith.

"Correct," said Chiun. "Do you have some?"

"No," Smith said.

"Could you get us a bottle?"

"I don't think they sell bottles. Why?"

"I have been very busy practicing tolerance for inferior peoples quite a while. If you notice, I have not mentioned that either of you are white. This is part of my new program to tolerate the inferior of the world. But if we got some of this DNA, we could change the whites and the blacks to yellow. Then we could change the level to Korean. And then improve that to North Korean. Do you follow me?"

"So far," said Smith.

"Then we could refine all those North Koreans into the best of what anyone can or could aspire to be. A person from Sinanju. Do not be overwhelmed, Emperor, but is that not a wonder to conjure?"

"Yeah, Smitty," Remo said. "Just think. You'll have four billion. Just like Chiun."

"I can't get any DNA," Smith said rapidly.

Remo laughed. "He'll settle for a centrifuge," he said.

Chiun said even though he was tolerant, it was still just like whites to fritter away what was probably their last chance to improve themselves.

He told Remo in Korean that would be the theme of his next book.

"*Next* book?" asked Remo. "Where's your last book?"

"I have decided not to waste it on you people. You

180

wouldn't appreciate it. But this next book might bring you to your senses."

"When are you going to write it?" asked Remo.

"I would have had it well underway by now if I had not had to waste so much time on you. If you will just leave me alone and keep things quiet, I will finish it in no time."

"I'll do my best," Remo said.

"That will not be good enough," said Chiun. "It never is."

ALL NEW·DYNAMITE SERIES

THE DESTROYER

by Richard Sapir & Warren Murphy

CURE, the world's most secret crime-fighting organization created the perfect weapon —Remo Williams—man programmed to become a cold, calculating death machine. The super man of the 70s!

Order		Title	Book No.	Price
_____	# 1	Created, The Destroyer	P361	$1.25
_____	# 2	Death Check	P362	$1.25
_____	# 3	Chinese Puzzle	P363	$1.25
_____	# 4	Mafia Fix	P364	$1.25
_____	# 5	Dr. Quake	P365	$1.25
_____	# 6	Death Therapy	P366	$1.25
_____	# 7	Union Bust	P367	$1.25
_____	# 8	Summit Chase	P368	$1.25
_____	# 9	Murder's Shield	P369	$1.25
_____	#10	Terror Squad	P370	$1.25
_____	#11	Kill or Cure	P371	$1.25
_____	#12	Slave Safari	P372	$1.25
_____	#13	Acid Rock	P373	$1.25
_____	#14	Judgment Day	P303	$1.25
_____	#15	Murder Ward	P331	$1.25
_____	#16	Oil Slick	P418	$1.25
_____	#17	Last War Dance	P435	$1.25
_____	#18	Funny Money	P538	$1.25
_____	#19	Holy Terror	P640	$1.25
_____	#20	Assassins Play-Off	P708	$1.25
_____	#21	Deadly Seeds	P760	$1.25
_____	#22	Brain Drain	P805	$1.25
_____	#23	Child's Play	P842	$1.25
_____	#24	King's Curse	P879	$1.25

TO ORDER

Please check the space next to the book/s you want, send this order form together with your check or money order, include the price of the book/s and 25¢ for handling and mailing, to:

PINNACLE BOOKS, INC. / P.O. Box 4347
Grand Central Station / New York, N. Y. 10017

☐ Check here if you want a free catalog.

I have enclosed $_____ check_____ or money order_____ as payment in full. No C.O.D.'s.

Name_____

Address_____

City_____State_____Zip_____
(Please allow time for delivery)

THE PENETRATOR

by Lionel Derrick

Mark Hardin. Discharged from the army, after service in Vietnam. His military career was over. But *his* war was just beginning. His reason for living and reason for dying became the same—to stamp out crime and corruption wherever he finds it. He is deadly; he is unpredictable; and he is dedicated. He is The Penetrator!

Read all of him in: